BOUDOIR BEDLAM

"You do anything but breathe, Mister Morgan, and you'll be all over that bed." The man who spoke was wearing a business suit. So were the two men with the shotguns. The bathroom door opened and Morgan tensed. He was ready to roll to his right when Emmy screamed. It might just give him the time he needed. The Colt was ten feet away.

"My God," Emmy said, "you sure as hell took long enough." She was fully dressed. The man without the shotgun smiled weakly.

BUCKSKIN #16

WINCHESTER VALLEY

KIT DALTON

LEISURE BOOKS NEW YORK CITY

A LEISURE BOOK®

July 2004

Published by

Dorchester Publishing Co., Inc.
200 Madison Avenue
New York, NY 10016

ISBN 0-8439-2463-2

Visit us on the web at www.dorchesterpub.com.

BUCKSKIN #16

WINCHESTER VALLEY

Dedicated to
Robert Vaughan, fellow writer who gave me a boost
when it was badly needed.

1

Lee Morgan liked the cool, slick feel of the silk sheets against his bare skin. He pulled the top sheet up high enough to cover his privates and smiled as he wondered why he'd bothered. After all, he'd been with Emmy for two nights. She knew every inch of his body. His modesty suddenly seemed a little ridiculous.

Morgan was still somewhat in awe of his recent streak of good luck. He rarely got anything he didn't work or fight for . . . most of the time at risk of his life. In this instance, a sick horse had been responsible. The animal had taken ill while stabled in Manhattan, Kansas. After it died, Morgan took the last of his cash to buy a stage ticket to Denver. It was on that stage that he met Emmy.

Emilia Christine Venable! Slim of waist, full of bosom, dark haired, dark eyed and very, very rich. She was the daughter of a Colorado Senator and gold baron. How ironic! Morgan had been bound for Denver to look up an old saddle companion and put the touch on him. Suddenly, there was Emmy. She introduced him to a lifestyle he'd rarely known.

They were quartered in the fabulous Windsor Hotel at 16th and Larimer. They had a four-room private suite, the best food and liquor money could buy, and all the privacy Morgan could handle. He hadn't even bothered to contact Jim Buttrey. He'd do that when Emmy tired of him. And he was sure she would.

"Do you like it?" Morgan blinked, his attention abruptly brought back to his present circumstance. He looked up. Emmy was wearing a black, lacy Merry Widow corset. It pushed her breasts up and together. Their creamy flesh overflowed its top. Morgan eyed them, then let his gaze trace the long, shapely legs from ankle to thigh. He licked his lips in anticipation of again visiting what was between them.

"I like it," he said. "But I like what's in it even better." Emmy smiled, coyly. She let her hands slide along her thighs and waist and then paused teasingly beneath her breasts.

"I'm glad, but champagne first. Right?" Morgan didn't care. He shrugged his reply. "The boy will be here with it in a minute. Let him in. I just want to add a finishing touch." She winked and wiggled her bottom as she disappeared into the water closet. Morgan shook his head in wonderment. She did have a way of renewing his thirst . . . no matter how short a time between trips to the well. A knock at the door.

"Yeah . . . c'mon in." Morgan scooted up a little so that he might rest his back against the headboard. The door opened, Morgan looked over. He was staring into the business end of two shotguns.

"You do anything but breathe, Mister Morgan, and you'll be all over that bed." The man who spoke was wearing a business suit. So were the two men with the shotguns. The bathroom door opened and Morgan tensed. He was ready to roll to his right when Emmy screamed. It might just give him the time he needed. The Colt was ten feet away.

"My God," Emmy said, "you sure as hell *took* long enough." She was fully dressed. The man without the shotgun smiled, weakly.

"Sorry," he offered. Morgan's mouth was half open. He'd been taken! Set up! It didn't happen often but when it did, it was *all* the way. "We had to be sure . . . absolutely sure about our man. Your father insisted on that."

"But he didn't give a damn that his daughter might have to go to bed with the man . . . right one or not."

"You don't look any the worse for wear," Emmy sneered. She walked to the nearby desk, picked up an envelope and took it to the man, pushing by him as she held it out. She got to the door and then turned back.

"Only one night was part of the set-up, Morgan . . . if that's any consolation." Morgan didn't respond. He was pondering how long he might have left to live.

"Get dressed, Morgan, we've got an appointment. Get out of the bed on *this* side. Charlie," the man continued, addressing the man on his right, "get his clothes and bring them over here." Charlie did as he was told. So did Morgan.

2

The mansion was pretentious, with ornate iron deer and marble statuary gracing the front lawn. Morgan caught a glimpse of a private coach being readied for a trip. As the surrey pulled up in front of the portico, Morgan saw the wrought iron fancy work between the center pillars. It was woven into a name and verified what he already suspected:

Venable

Morgan was ushered into the library and ordered to sit. One man accompanied him while the others took up guard duties nearby. A few moments later, a tall, graying gentleman entered. He was wearing a monogrammed silk shirt, broadcloth suit and a cravat held in place with a diamond stickpin.

"Give him back his gun, Mister Denton." Denton assumed a look of surprise but didn't move. "I said, give the man his gun."

"Senator . . . this man is . . ."

"I know who he is . . . and what. Now sir, give him

his gun." Denton gritted his teeth but he complied. The tall man then moved to a nearby liquor cabinet, poured two shots of whisky and walked over to Morgan. "I'm Senator Charles Wingate Venable, Mister Morgan. I must apologize for the circumstances under which we are meeting."

Morgan accepted the whiskey and downed it in a single gulp. "Under any other circumstances, I doubt that we would meet at all."

"Perhaps not, but I'm certain you must have many questions."

"Only one for right now," Morgan said. "What kind of a man would use his daughter the way you did?"

Venable assumed a rather quizzical expression. Denton took two steps in Morgan's direction, but Venable held up his hand.

"Hate is a strong motivator, sir. All I ask is that you do not judge either of us until you've heard the facts."

"Shotguns pointed at my belly make me very hard of hearing," Morgan said.

"Then you will listen?"

"Why not? The whisky's good and the last few days at the Windsor must have some price on them. Listening seems cheap enough."

"Mister Denton," Venable said, "you and your men go on to the dining room. They will serve you breakfast." Denton started to speak but the Senator held up his hand. "I'll be just fine, don't worry." Morgan could tell by Denton's expression how the man felt but, one way or another, Denton was on Venable's payroll. He did what he was told.

"Another whisky, Mister Morgan?"

"Why don't you just bring the bottle over. Interruptions are distracting." Morgan strapped on his rig, checked the Colt for load and then pondered an escape through the French doors. Venable caught the look.

"I dare say you'd get off the grounds, Mister Morgan . . . but you'd never get out of Denver."

"And after I listen?"

"I'll speak frankly, sir. As of this moment, you're facing charges of kidnapping and rape. Your life depends on those charges never leaving this room. That, sir, is up to you."

Morgan downed a whiskey and started to pour another. He looked at Senator Venable, smiled and put the glass on the table. Then he tipped the bottle up and took several good-sized swallows.

"Do you always drink this heavily, Mister Morgan?"

"No, no. Just on those days when I'm facing kidnap and rape charges." The men eyed each other for a moment . . . a considering of strengths and weaknesses. Morgan half smiled. "I could add murder to the list," he said, "it wouldn't go any harder on me."

"I don't like this," Venable said. His face contorted and his tone had changed. He meant it. "I just can't run the risk of being turned down."

"For *what*?"

Venable walked to his desk, pulled a *Wanted* poster from a drawer and handed it to Morgan. "I want you to hunt down and arrest this man . . . or kill him." Morgan looked at the name. It was Henry Jared.

"Doc Henry?" Morgan laughed. "Hang me, Senator. It'll be a damn site quicker."

"I know you're not afraid of him, Morgan. I know you faced him down, and I don't know anyone else who has. If you do . . . get him here and you're free to go."

"I can give you the names of a dozen men who faced Doc . . . but you wouldn't want them here. They're all in pine boxes."

"You're not."

"And you don't have your facts as straight as you think."

"It's all right here, Morgan." Venable held up an envelope. Morgan recognized it as the one Emmy had given to Denton earlier.

"And that says I faced down Doc Henry?"

"You don't remember? Laramie? Two, maybe three years ago?"

"I don't remember because it never happened, Venable. The man I faced was Doc Henry's brother, Johnny. I've still got a chunk of lead in a rib bone to remind me."

"No matter, Morgan. The fact is . . . you're not afraid of him . . . either of them. Are you?"

"Makes no difference," Morgan replied. "I don't intend to go looking for trouble. Plenty of it comes my way without looking."

"How much, Morgan? What will it take to buy your gun?"

"Save it, Senator. If you'd have thought you

could buy my gun, you wouldn't have gone to all this trouble."

"I'd prefer to pay you. Officially, of course but . . . well, I have to have some assurances."

"Here's one for you Senator. I assure you I won't go looking for Doc Henry Jared."

The door opened and both men turned. Emmy Venable walked in.

"Emilia," her father said, "I told you . . ."

"I know what you told me, father, but after what I did, I've earned the right to be here."

"For what it's worth, lady," Morgan said, cynically, "you did a helluva job on me."

"I told you, Morgan, only the first night was part of the plan."

"*Emilia!* Surely you didn't . . ."

"Don't sound so shocked, father. You can't be that naive. How did you expect me to hold his attention for three days?"

"Your money of course. The hotel. Your *name.*"

Emmy's eyes suddenly filled with tears and she assumed an almost hateful expression. She spat the words at her father. "All that didn't help Carla did it? Or Carl? Or Momma . . . none of it helped them, *Senator* Venable."

Morgan realized a more complex issue was at stake than some politician wanting to gain a vote or two by ending the career of a notorious gunman. There was emotion here . . . family emotion.

"Just what interest does a millionaire politician have in a man like Doc Henry?" Morgan could see tears now in the Senator's eyes.

"He . . . he killed my family, Morgan. Or at least

he was responsible for their deaths. My other daughter, Carla. My son. God! Poor Carl. He had to watch . . . Carla with . . . with those men. He tried to stop them . . . to stand up against them."

"And your wife?"

Venable blew his nose, downed a swallow of whisky and regained some of his composure. "She put a gun to her head."

"How in the hell did Doc Henry's men ever get that Goddam close to the family of a man like you?"

"They were on the way to the wedding of the daughter of the Mexican Ambassador, Senor Juan Diego Valesquez. His home is near Juarez."

"Publicity?"

"A great deal of it, Morgan. It was to have been a major breakthrough in our relationship with Mexico. A new beginning. Emilia and I were in Washington."

"And you let the rest of your family make that trip without escort?"

"Of course not! As a matter of fact, there was a troop of Cavalry and the usual personal body guards. More than twenty men all together. The party was attacked by a band of renegade Apaches. The Indians traded the survivors, which included my family, for guns."

"From Doc Henry?"

"Yes. He's been running guns to them for a long time. They've been stirring up much of the trouble between our country and Mexico. The fight has been over who is responsible for bringing them to justice. The Apaches ignore the international boundary."

"Yeah. Since they owned all of it once, I can see

where they would. I still can't figure why Doc didn't demand payment from you, though."

"He did! Unfortunately, a hot-headed army Lieutenant tried to take action on his own before I even knew about the events or the ransom."

Now Emmy joined in. She was no longer crying, she was *mad*, damned mad.

"Doc Henry turned Carla over to his men. When they were through with her, they gave her back to the Apaches."

"And just how and when did you find out about all of this?"

"Only a month ago, Morgan. Until then, we didn't know the fates of any of them."

"And me, Mr. Venable? Just how in the hell do I fit in?"

"There was a man who once worked for the Pinkertons. When I was elected, he went to work for me. He undertook the job of getting the truth, paying the ransom, whatever he had to do."

"And where is he?"

"Dead, I suppose. I'm not certain." Venable took another envelope from his desk. This one was thicker, its contents dog-eared. He handed it to Morgan. "Read it, Morgan. It's his complete report."

Morgan read. The author had been thorough. Sickeningly so where it related to Venable's family. There had been many other victims too, over a long period of time. Women and young girls from emigrant trains headed west, mining camps, even small towns sacked. The gang, growing in numbers and in the vileness of their atrocities, had become an empire of evil. Somewhere they hid themselves away between attacks. A fortress, probably impregnable. Morgan had read enough. He started to hand the papers back. Venable shook his head.

"The last page, Morgan . . . read it . . . read the signature." Morgan read again.

> I was never able to pinpoint the exact location of Jared's stronghold, but there is someone who knows and there is one man who might get in alone. He is Lee Morgan. Have him contact Irish Molly. This is probably my last report, sir. I've been discovered.
>
> J.B.

Morgan looked up, frowning. "J.B.?"

"James Buttrey, Mister Morgan, the man you were coming to see."

"I'll be damned!" Morgan looked at Emmy. "Jim Buttrey, a Pinkerton agent. This has been a week of surprises."

"Do you know this woman, Morgan? This Irish Molly?"

"Yeah, I know her. She runs a whore house in Creede."

"And just how would she know where Doc Henry's gang is holed up?" Emmy asked.

"She's known Doc for years. He likes his women and he likes to take care of the men who ride with him."

"Will you take the job, Morgan?" It was Emmy asking. No threat now. In fact, more a plea.

"How can I do what Jim Buttrey, the U.S.

Cavalry and a Senator with a million dollars couldn't do?"

"One man Morgan . . . alone. That's what Buttrey said."

"*He* was alone."

"But he was . . . involved."

"Working for you, you mean?"

"I mean . . . Jim was in love with my other daughter."

"Lost his edge," Morgan said, almost in a whisper.

"What? What was that about an edge? Jim mentioned that once."

"You ought to know about that, Senator. Politics is full of it. It's what you've got . . . wealth and power. For Buttrey . . . for me, the tools are different but the edge is the same. Lose it and you'll die."

"Have you got it, Morgan? I mean in this case . . . with Doc Henry?"

"Mebbe. If Irish Molly will help, just mebbe."

"Morgan," Senator Venable said, softly, "I'm sorry . . . terribly sorry for the way I got you here. Ashamed too. And the threats . . . forget them. I want you to do this job officially . . . as a Pinkerton agent. That way, Jared and any of his gang members who might survive can be legally tried and hanged." Venable paused. Morgan knew he wasn't a man accustomed to apologizing or backing down. Venable stood up and pulled himself to his full height. "Unofficially, I'll pay you any amount you ask. Just name it."

"I've got a dodger or two hanging over me Senator. No murders, just mistakes . . . small ones. I don't like them dogging me. Wipe the slate clean . . . if I make it. Clear them for me. Pay my expenses. You can call what it's worth to you after that."

"Then you'll . . ." Emmy looked up now too, her eyes wide. Morgan looked from one to the other.

"For Jim Buttrey," he said.

3

Creede, Colorado had the dubious distinction of being called "Hell at Heaven's Gate." It was a lawless, rip-roaring mining town some ten thousand feet above sea level. Just to the north were the La Garita Mountains and the south, the San Juans. Northwest lay the Spring Creek Pass, primary access into the wilds of the Uncompahgre Valley. Few men had reason to ride in there. No one came to Creede itself without a damned good reason. Most of those who did were seeking their fortunes. The gold and silver mines were some of the best producers in the territory. Then too, there were those who followed the men who were following the rainbow.

Creede had once boasted a sheriff and two deputies. They now reposed on Calvary Hill. Legend had it that Creede had once enjoyed three summer months without a single shooting. The reason was a visitor from back east. He agreed to wear the tin star of the law in exchange for room and board. At summer's end, Dr. John Holliday quit Creede and returned to warmer climes.

Lee Morgan came to Creede by stage. Butterfield

ran two into the town; they tried to time the once-a-month runs to accommodate passengers going in either direction. Most of the time there were two or three day lay-overs. The runs were rugged enough given the country. Men like Doc Henry made them more so.

Senator Venable had advanced Morgan $1,500 for expenses. He was ready to outfit himself in Creede and maintain a low profile until he could develop a plan, hopefully with Irish Molly's help.

Morgan was surprised at the growth since his last visit. He'd come to Creede then following a trail he hoped would lead him to his father. Creede had often offered respite to Buckskin Frank Leslie when he was alive.

Morgan had no trouble finding Irish Molly's place. It too had grown, nearly tripled in size. He stood in the street and read the sign, which appeared to be fairly new.

Irish Molly's
Keno   Poker   21   Whisky   Beer
Women
If you're honest . . . you're
Welcome!
If not . . . you're
dead!

Morgan grinned. He could hear Molly speaking the words with that deep, Irish brogue. Her place had a fancy facade, covered half a block and sported three entrances. The center one, into the dining room, was high with fancy cut glass windows. On either side were bat wing doors leading into the casino and the saloon. Upstairs was Molly's private quarters and the rooms of pleasure. Molly's place, like Creede itself, never closed.

Morgan, noting the two armed men at each entrance, opted to enter the casino. Inside, he found himself confronted by another armed man.

"Check your weapons with the young lady." Morgan glanced around. No one else was carrying a gun. He nodded.

"Now, sir, your pleasure?"

"I'm here to see the owner. Just tell her Lee is here and that it's very important."

"I don't believe Miss O'Flynn is up for the day yet, sir. I will see to it she gets your message, however. Meantime, take your stage ticket stub into the dining room and enjoy Irish Molly's free breakfast." Morgan's eyebrows raised. He was impressed. He remembered Molly talking about something like that a long time ago.

"Thanks," he said. "I'll do that."

The breakfast lived up to Molly's promise. A sizeable cut of steak, some potatoes, flap jacks, and all the coffee a man could hold. The steak was actually antelope or venison, and sometimes even bear meat. Honest to God beef steak was at a premium and Molly saved that for her dining room dinner business. Morgan was just finishing his third cup of coffee when he heard the rustle of a satin dress. He saw the hem of the Emerald green garb and the slim ankles below it. He looked up.

"As the Good Lawrd is me witness, if it ain't Lee Morgan himself." The brogue was still there, the face pixie-like, the hair a flame red. Molly's eyes matched her gown. She pushed aside the tin plate, leaned down and gave Morgan a long, hard kiss. He nearly choked on the coffee he had not yet swallowed.

"You can still take my breath away, Molly."

She sat opposite him, eyeing his every feature and smiling. "You've not changed a bloody bit. I should be angry with you. You promised a letter a month you did. Blarney! I've not heard from you since you rode out. Let's see now, that's been . . ."

"Let's just say it's been too long, Molly, shall we?"

"That it has, Morgan." She tilted her head and cocked one eye at him. "An' what brings you back, I'll be askin'?"

"This will tell you as much as I could." Morgan handed her Jim Buttrey's letter. She read it and then looked up. "Did you see him, Molly . . . lately, I mean?"

"We buried him Thursday week."

"Who did it?"

"Who knows?"

"You do, Molly. Was it Doc Henry or one of his gunnies?"

"Does it matter? He's gone, he is, an' nobody can get them all, can they now?"

"I'm going to try, Molly," Morgan said, "but I need your help."

"You'll not be gettin' it, Mahrgan. I'll not send you to your death."

"If you don't tell me what you know, Molly girl, that may be exactly what you'll do. See, I'm going to find him, with or without you."

"You're a damned, bloody fool you are. Nobody can take Doc Henry. Most can't even find him."

"But you can." She was already shaking her head.

"Not even me," Molly said. "Not unless Doc wants me to. He hasn't. Not for a long time now."

"Jim said you knew."

"I know that Doc holes up in the Uncompahgre Valley. That's the same as tellin' you there's gold in the Rockies. There's a site more mountains than there is gold. A man could ride for a year up there an' niver seen another human bein'."

"Then," Morgan said, standing up, "I'd best get started." Molly reached out and gripped Morgan's arm. "Wait! Stay the night!"

"With you?"

"You owe me, Mahrgan. After all, you niver wrote."

" 'Til tonight then, Molly."

Morgan picked up his rig but left the Winchester checked. He went first to the Creede livery stable, where a hulk of a man greeted him.

"I'm looking to buy a horse. You sellin'?"

"Fer packin' er ridin'?"

"One of each," Morgan said. He'd learned that the death of his riding mare in Kansas had also been part of Venable's set-up. It was one reason for the sizeable advance of expense money.

"I got pack animals, mister. Best ridin' mounts you'll have to get from the Halsteads."

"And where are they?" The man pointed south. "How far?"

"Two . . . three miles, mebbe." The big man took Morgan to the rear of the stable and pointed to a corral. "Six or seven good pack animals out there. Take yore pick."

Morgan found a good, strong pack pony. He then

went to the mercantile and bought his supplies, leaving them until he could return later. He also bought a saddle. Then he rode the pack pony to the Halstead ranch.

"The livery man told me you sold horses."

"The best in the mountains, mister. I'm Luke Halstead. This is muh daddy's spread. You lookin' for a runner or a climber?"

"You got one that'll do both?"

"Sure do." He eyed Morgan carefully. "Most men can't afford 'em."

"I'll pay cash, right now!"

The man shrugged. "Got a big roan gelding out back. Runs like the wind, climbs like a mountain goat. Fella what owned him got himself kilt a week or so back. We bought the horse so there'd be buryin' money."

"You happen to know the name of the man who owned him?"

"Nope. That make a difference to you?"

"Not really. Let's have a look."

The horse was obviously a good one. He'd been treated well and seemed to take to Morgan quickly.

"You can saddle 'im up if you want. See how he gets on with you."

"No need. I'll take him." Morgan paid Halstead and while Halstead was getting the paper, Morgan checked the horse over. He found what he was looking for . . . a brand. It was simple and personal. The letters were J.B.

Morgan was looking over several other animals when Halstead returned.

"You change your mind, mister?"

"No."

25

"You lookin' for somethin' special?"

"You get all your horses the way you got the roan?"

"I don't figure that to be your business, mister. They're all bought, paid for, an' I got papers."

"And you don't care where they come from?"

"Nope. Don't care where they're goin' neither . . . or the men who rides 'em."

"You bought any horses from a man called Jared? Doc Henry Jared?"

"You're pushin', mister . . . way too hard." Morgan heard a twig snap just behind him. He crouched, spun and leveled the Colt at the man who stepped on it. The motion was fluid . . . all done at once.

"You're mighty edgy, mister."

"When somebody gets behind me, I tend to get that way."

"You'll find no trouble here, mister . . . unless you make it. I'm Henry Halstead. This is my place. I buy horses from any man who'll sell 'em to me at a fair price. That's my business. Where the horses come from in the first place, *ain't*!"

Morgan rode away but he wasn't easy with it. He'd found three animals with cavalry brands, two others with private brands the same as Jim Buttrey's, and one Indian pony.

The curtain swayed to the night breeze. The air was crisp at this altitude, even in the dead of summer. Morgan slipped out of his long-johns and sat on the edge of the bed. In the dim light, Molly came from the next room, naked.

Her breasts were not large but they were firm and jutted upwards at the nipples. The little buds were hard and a soft pink in color. Her pubic hair was not the flaming red Morgan remembered. It was softer in color and seemed less than he recalled . . . but no less inviting.

"Kiss me, Mahrgan . . . the way you used to." She stood in front of him, her legs slightly apart. She clamped her hands together, behind her head. Morgan reached up and tweaked the nipples, rubbed them and filled his hands with the rubbery softness of Molly's tits.

"Stay still," he said. "Stay still . . . no matter what."

Morgan's tongue circled Molly's navel. She sucked in her breath but she didn't move. He pulled at her waist and she leaned forward just a little. He licked each nipple until they were as hard as rocks. He could feel Molly's body tensing against the urge to move. His hands tightened around her ass and he let his tongue work nearer to her pussy.

"Oooh Gawd . . . it's been so long . . . ooh."

"Shh!" Morgan found the slit. It was slick, wet . . . almost pulsating. He teased her, avoiding her clitoris. She moved ever so slightly and he tightened his hands against her as a warning.

He flicked at her love bud, even closing his lips around it briefly. Then he'd stop and repeat the procedure again. Molly's body was covered with goose pimples. Her eyes were closed and she was biting her lip to keep from screaming with the pleasure of it all.

Morgan pushed her back, gently. Now he dropped to his knees and buried his face in her softness . . . his tongue found her clitoris. The fingers of his hands were on her nipples. The sensations were

27

shooting through her body in waves, each moment increasing in momentum. He licked faster and faster ... she moaned ... she stiffened ... she thrust her hips forward ... hard! Morgan stopped!

"On the bed," he said. His voice was firm, commanding. Molly obeyed. She knew what to do. She got up on her knees, spread them wide apart and then reached behind her and gripped the headboard with both hands. Morgan got on his back, his face beneath her pussy. "Lower yourself," he ordered. She did. Morgan's tongue went to work again. This time, he'd attack her clitoris, then thrust his tongue up, inside her. Again, repeating the process over and over.

"I can't Mahrgan ... I can't take it ... oooh God. God ..."

"Quiet!"

"Oh *please* ... please, Mahrgan. . . ." He stopped completely. Molly's breathing was the only sound. It was heavy and rapid.

"Are you ready to be quiet, Molly ... or do you want it the hard way?"

"Oh no ... please. It's just that it's been so long ... I ..."

"Which is it going to be Molly?"

"I'll be quiet ... I swear it."

"And still?"

"Yes ... I'll not move again, Mahrgan."

Once again, Molly lowered herself to Morgan's tongue. He couldn't help but smile to himself. He knew he was torturing her but it was the most pleasant torture he could imagine. He continued to tease her for another ten minutes. Even in the cool night air, Molly's body glistened with sweat. Finally, Morgan stopped.

"You were a pretty good girl this time. Lay down." Molly moved quickly and Morgan positioned himself so that his cock touched her lips. She licked the tip, the shaft, the swollen head and finally took it, deep, into her mouth and throat. Gurgling sounds punctuated her effort. It had been a long time for Morgan as well. He suddenly pulled back, slipped atop her and thrust himself deep inside her.

"Don't tease me anymore," she cried. He didn't. Their bodies became a single, human piston until Molly exploded inside. Morgan was only a split-second behind her. Their moans and words were lost in the fiery passion of climax. Molly seemed insatiable but finally, she too fell limp beneath him.

"You're still the best I've ever had," she finally said. Morgan knew she meant it. He always felt guilty about not saying the same thing. It wasn't that he couldn't have said it . . . Morgan just wasn't certain it was true. Instead, he kissed her.

4

Morgan had only the most vague recollection of Molly's departure the following morning. He was very much aware, however, that he had slept well past his usual time. He was fully dressed, save for his shirt, when Molly returned. She was followed by a man with a huge tray of food.

"We got some talkin' to do," she said. "May as well do it over a good breakfast." After the hired hand left, Molly walked over and kissed Morgan, long but soft. "Top o' the marnin' to you."

"And to you, Molly my girl," Morgan replied. He made a half hearted attempt at an Irish brogue. It didn't work. Molly laughed.

Throughout breakfast, Molly spoke of many things. Among them old times she remembered with Morgan and Jim Buttrey. By the last of the coffee, her mood had turned solemn. Morgan didn't push her but he didn't have to wait long.

"Charlie Bojack rode in this marnin'. He's a gunny. Works for Doc Henry. He brought this." Molly reached inside the top of her blouse and extracted a folded paper. She handed it to Morgan. He opened and read it.

Molly,
    I know you won't come personal, but I'd like to ask you anyways. My men need some ladies. Nine will do. $200 a girl for two nights. Meet Charlie at the pass in five days. He'll bring you in.

My love . . .

Doc

"You've got something in that scheming red head of yours. What is it?"

"I don't have nine girls here that I can spare. I run a small house down at South Fork. You came through it comin' in." Morgan nodded. "I can close it down for a week or so. I got five girls there. You can go get 'em, Mahrgan. Ride out tonight. There's an old stage coach down there. You can bring them and yourself back in it. Then," she said, smiling, "you'll be workin' for *me*. Just make certain Charlie Bojack don't see you today."

"Whoa, Molly. I can't risk other people going after Doc. He finds me out . . . or someone else does . . ."

"It's a chance we'll have to take, Mahrgan. There's no other way to get into Doc's camp."

"*We?*"

"This is a trip I'll be makin' too."

"Not on your life, Molly."

"Then we'll be strikin' no bargain."

"I don't need your bargain, Molly. I can follow Bojack and your girls from a nice safe distance. I'll get in."

"Not with busted legs you won't, and if you won't be dealin' me in, I'll see to it that's what you end up with." Morgan knew Molly meant what she said. She had enough men to get the job done.

"What changed your mind, Molly? You didn't want any part of Doc Henry yesterday."

"With this note from Doc, we got a chance to get in. I've got some good men that'll come in mighty handy when the shootin' starts and then there's Jaimie boy. Cold dead he is. Sod coverin' 'im up 'cause o' Doc Henry Jared. I don't need any more reasons."

"Fair enough."

"Not quite, Mahrgan. I got a feelin', deep down, that Jaimie's shootin is not your only reason. Am I right?"

"You are. Money is the other one."

"That's all?"

"Isn't that enough?"

Morgan whiled away the day in Molly's casino. One of the girls kept Charlie Bojack occupied for most of it. Toward sundown, Morgan made his way to the livery. He had just finished saddling the roan when he heard the creak of the door. He stepped back into the shadows.

"Your daddy ain't gonna like this, Luke. Not one little bit he ain't."

"Don't you worry none about my daddy. Just you git up in the loft and make sure we get this Morgan fella alive. He's got some questions to answer."

Morgan moved quietly until he could peer between two boards. He could see Luke Halstead's outline by the light from the door behind him. The other man was half way up a ladder to the loft. Morgan didn't want any shooting . . . if he could help it. He found an old horseshoe and tossed it into the air, behind him. It fell into a stall several feet away with a rattle and spooked a horse.

Luke Halstead, shotgun in hand, made a dash for the other end of the livery barn. When he got even with Morgan, Morgan thrust his boot out and Luke went ass over appetite.

Morgan planted the butt of his Colt on the back of Luke's head and there was only a soft grunt. The other man had jumped from the ladder when the horseshoe hit and was frozen to the spot.

"You come tend to your friend here," Morgan said. "I'm riding out of Creede and I'd like to do it with no dead men left behind me. I hope you'll cooperate."

"Yes, sir, yes, sir. You'll git no argument out o' me." The man moved slowly up to where Morgan stood over Luke. Morgan backed the roan out of the stall, mounted and then told the man to lie face down and stay put. The man complied. Minutes later, Morgan was galloping south.

Luke Halstead was scared. He'd always promised Doc Henry that he'd handle any problems at his end. So far, Luke's father had believed the stories he'd been told about the origin of the stock Luke bought. He loved his son and he trusted him. Jim Buttrey had come snooping around the Halstead stock too. Luke had handled that . . . with a shotgun. Lee Morgan, if he was more than he appeared, would be another matter.

"I want that sonuvabitch dead," Luke said. He

was still groggy.

"He tol' me he was ridin' out o' Creede. Maybe we'd best let it be, Luke. We don't want Doc Henry on our asses do we?" Luke looked up. His little friend was right. Luke nodded.

"Yeah, okay for right now. But if that bastard comes back, I'm taking 'im out."

South Fork was a whore house which also happened to provide a livery barn, mercantile, stage stop and five saloons. The only women in the settlement were those of ill repute. Most of the men were either on the run or in between illegal activities.

Morgan contacted the girl named Gretchen who ran Molly's house in the community. She told him she'd have the girls ready to leave by the following morning. He lined up the stage coach and then found his way to the most raucous of South Fork's saloons. He was soon immersed in a six-man stud poker game.

By midnight, though down about two hundred dollars, Morgan was still in the game. Now he was one of only four men playing. He had barely noticed the entry of two new faces in the saloon, but he had a feeling he was being watched. After a win, Morgan stood up and announced he was going to get himself a cold beer. As he turned to walk to the bar, one of the two new faces appeared in front of him.

"I been tryin' to figure you, mister, and now I don't have to anymore. You're Lee Morgan." Morgan eyed the man carefully but he was also aware of the movement of the second man. Off to his right, the man had circled and now flanked him.

"You find something wrong with who I am?"

"You gunned down my brother," the man said. "It was in Cheyenne, a year back."

Morgan remembered. "Davy Wickett wasn't it?"

"Yeah. I'm Tom and that there's my brother Joad."

The Wickett boys were sometime bounty hunters and all-time bastards. They had never brought a man in alive and most of the dead ones had been shot in the back.

"You should have told your little brother who he'd be facing. Maybe he'd still be alive," Morgan said. The man's face twisted into a scowl and he stepped back. Morgan could detect a similar move by the man to his far right. Chairs scraped across the old wooden floor as men jumped up and scurried for neutral corners. The saloon girls were huddled in a little knot at the end of the bar.

"I heard you back shot 'im, Morgan."

"You heard wrong."

"I don't think so," the man replied, pausing only long enough to curl his lips into a sneering smile, "but either way, I'm sayin' you did."

"You're a liar, Wickett." Morgan's voice was soft but his demeanor displayed his readiness to back the allegation. He punctuated his words with a slight shift in his own position. He was now facing in a diagonal direction between the two men. He could see both but faced neither head-on.

"You ain't good enough to take us both," Tom Wickett said.

"Then I'll make damned sure you're the volunteer for the one I do get." As Morgan spoke, his eyes shifted, for just a split second, to Tom Wickett's six gun. It was an old Navy Colt, hung low on the man's leg and tied down. Morgan could take this man in a heartbeat. He couldn't see Joad Wickett's rig so he'd have to take him out first.

Just as Morgan had anticipated, it was Joad who made the first move, and it was fast. Morgan drew, dropped into a semi-crouch and felt the sting of splintering wood strike his right cheek. His own bullet had already struck Joad Wickett, killing him instantly. The Bisley's barrel was levelled at Tom Wickett's heart when a shotgun went off. It nearly tore Tom's arm from the socket and Morgan's own reflexes precluded stopping his own action. Tom didn't feel much pain from the shotgun blast. He was dead a split second later.

Morgan's brain relayed still another signal to his deadly right arm. Maybe the shotgun was meant for him. The Colt found its target even before Morgan's eyes could focus on it. There, half way up the staircase, stood Emmy Venable!

5

Emmy Venable refused to take "No" for an answer when she told Lee she planned to accompany him. The following morning, he purchased some chloroform from the town doctor, drugged Emmy and put her on the eastbound stage. By ten o'clock, he and his girls were well on their way back to Creede. Gretchen had opted to ride the shotgun seat.

"Molly told me she had five girls working for her. Where'd the extra come from?"

"I don't know," Gretchen replied. Morgan detected a deep, Southern drawn. "She just come bouncin' in one evenin', pretty as you please. Told me she'd work for room an' board. Ah don't think she's slept with a customer since she's been heah."

"She looks pretty young." Morgan turned and looked at Gretchen for her reaction. She was nodding.

"Ah think she said she was twenty but ah don't believe her. Why I doubt the girl's a day ovah seventeen."

"Yeah," Morgan said, "that'd by my guess." He

didn't know why but the presence of the extra girl, young as she was, bothered him. Morgan didn't like things out of the ordinary or last minute changes or new faces. At least, not while he was on a job that would probably bring him face to face with the likes of Doc Henry Jared.

The trip back to Creede was uneventful. Morgan had found himself some dude clothes, as he called them. Gretchen kept his things with her own, including his Colt. It wouldn't do for him to be seen wearing a gun while he was posing as pimp for Molly. He did carry a Derringer, but it afforded him no comfort.

Molly arranged for rooms for the girls, and Morgan stayed in her quarters. He'd simply stay out of sight for another day and then the little party would head northwest to meet Charlie Bojack. Molly was ready to bed down with Morgan again that night but, in a rare instance, Morgan wasn't.

"You're a mite fidgety," Molly said.

"You know anything about this extra girl?"

Molly looked surprised. She smiled. "Lee Morgan is worried about a snip of a girl? You've gone daft on me."

Morgan was on the bed, his back against the headboard, fingering the Derringer. He looked up at Molly, then back to the gun and said, "It isn't just the girl. Someone else showed up and I've got a hunch she'll show up again."

"She?"

Morgan nodded. "The daughter of the man I'm working for."

"And just who might that be?"

"I'd sooner not say," Morgan replied. "The less you know, the better."

"She after the same thing you are?" She paused and then placed more emphasis on her words. "Or is she after you?"

"Probably both." Now Morgan looked up. "But I told you before, I'm in this for the money." There was a knock at the door. Molly opened it, noting Morgan's reflexive tension. Morgan saw a tall, thin man dressed in a black suit, like an undertaker. Molly invited him in. It was then that Morgan spotted the man's gun.

"This is Trigg," she said. "He's my right hand." The tall man nodded when Morgan spoke to him. "He's a mute."

Morgan watched as the man scrawled a note to Molly. She read it, wrote a short reply and sent him on his way. Morgan saw that her face was somewhat paled.

"A problem?"

"Maybe a big one, Mahrgan. Doc Henry's brother is back in the territory. He was spotted in Durango four days ago."

"What was the note you wrote?"

"I told Trigg to put two o' my men to watchin' for him. He'd likely recognize you right off."

"More than just likely, Molly. He'd gun me in a heartbeat."

"My man figures Johnny Jared is the contact man for whatever scheme Doc Henry is into now. You know what it is?"

"Gun running to some Apache renegades."

"My men can take him out." Morgan shook his head. "Why not?"

"He's the only trail I've got right now. I can't be sure of finding out what I need to know in Doc Henry's camp . . . not even with the help of your girls. Johnny Jared is my back-up plan. I don't like it, but I'll have to use him."

"You sure you don't want me to have Johnny eliminated?"

"I'm sure."

'An' how about spendin' the night with you, Mahrgan? You still sure about *that*?"

Morgan eyed the swell of her breasts and the flair of her hips. He felt the tightness forming in his groin but it passed quickly. "Sorry," he said.

The sun was still struggling to climb above San Luis peak when the stagecoach reached the summit of Spring Creek pass. The horses' sides heaved under the weight of the load they pulled in the oxygen-thin air. The girls climbed down from the coach and gaped at the valley below them. It ran east and west for a hundred miles or more. Just a few miles to the northwest, it took a sharp rise up again, all the way to the summit of Slumgullion pass.

"You been to the Uncompahgre before?" Molly asked.

"Nope. Never had a reason."

"She's beautiful, Mahrgan . . . but she's deadly. In winter, the drifts get twenty feet deep and a blizzard can whip up in no time an' bury man an' beast alike."

"Yeah," Morgan said, taking in the entire panorama below him, "and it hides a few sidewinders as well . . . the two-legged variety."

"There's a man comin', Miss Molly." One of the girls was pointing down trail.

"Charlie Bojack," Molly said. She walked toward him, catching him about fifty yards from the coach. Charlie didn't look at her. His eyes were squinting into the morning sun, trying to identify Molly's male companion. " 'Lo, Charlie."

"Who's the dude?"

"Name's Wilfrid Butler. He runs some girls for me over in Walsenburg. Law got nasty and run 'im out. I brought 'im up to Creede to help out."

"Doc Henry ain't expectin' no dude."

"Doc Henry ain't expectin' me, Charlie. You want to tell 'im we're not comin' in because I had a dude with me?"

Charlie eyed her. Molly was smiling. Doc Henry would have Charlie's hide if he turned Molly down, dude or no dude. "Let's ride. We got some hard country to cover."

"Will we make it by dark?"

"We'll make it." Charlie looked toward Morgan again and then turned his horse and waited.

Charlie hadn't lied. The terrain was rugged. The trail led from the main road, itself only little more than a trail, down into the very depths of the Uncompahgre. It was early afternoon before they finally reached bottom. Another two hours passed as they followed a river along its course where it flowed down from the melted snows of Sheep mountain. Finally, Lake Fork river began a rushing trip into the final depths of the huge valley. Atop the last ridge before Doc Henry's hideaway, Charlie Bojack stopped the party.

"All guns git dumped right here. You got a gun, dude?"

"No, sir," Morgan said.

"I catch you lyin' to me an' I'll have your ass." He turned to Molly. "Any o' them girls got guns?"

She grinned. "They didn't come here to *shoot* anythin', Charlie." He nodded but Molly and Morgan could tell he wasn't completely convinced.

The coach finally came to a halt in front of a huge log house. It was, even by city standards, a fine residence. The door opened and out stepped Doc Henry Jared.

"I'll be a sumbitch," he shouted. "Molly!" He grabbed her around the waist and whirled her around several times, then he kissed her, hard. He finally put her back on the ground, pushed her away gently and made a wide, sweeping gesture with his arms. "Welcome to Winchester Valley," he said.

Morgan had taken note of every twist, turn and rock along the way. Even he was impressed. Doc Henry might only have nine men, but it would take a cavalry regiment to get to him. Besides, Morgan harbored no misconceptions about Doc Henry's men. They'd all be the best and he knew there would be more than any nine. These were his closest gang members, the leaders. Doc would have men riding in about every day before his next operation.

While Charlie directed Morgan and the girls to their quarters, Doc Henry met with Molly in the main house.

"I smell somethin' gone rotten," he said. "You never come before."

"I never had a reason before."

"You had me. Ain't that reason enough?"

"You can't buy me, Doc. I told you that before. I do business with them what can do business back."

"An' now you need ol' Doc Henry. Is that it?" She nodded. "What for?"

"Makin' money."

"I'm not in the whore business," Doc said.

"An' I want out of it. Runnin' guns to the Indians pays better from the look of it."

Doc Henry frowned and eyed Molly carefully. She had to tread ever so carefully, and she knew it. She struggled to keep smiling.

"What do you think you know?" he asked.

"The army is about to bring in twenty wagon loads o' guns . . . brand new guns. I know when and I know where. Seems to me that ought to be worth somethin' to you, Doc."

"Like what?"

"A third."

Doc laughed. "I got men up here what'd blow my head off if I give some whore a third o' their take."

"Winchester model '73's," Molly continued. She was acting as if Doc had said nothing. She walked to the window but she didn't turn to face him as she spoke. "They'd be worth fifty dollars each just to the Apache." Now she turned, quickly. "But to the Mexicans? You guess, Doc. A hundred apiece? A hundred and twenty-five maybe?"

"An' all in gold too," Doc said, sarcastically. He was surprised at Molly's response.

"Hell no, Doc. Silver! It's comin' out o' the ground at 225 ounces to the ton. The Mexicans will work for nothin' to mine it just to buy guns so's they can take over their government."

"An' you're tellin' me you know somebody who

can make that kind of deal." Doc got up. "That right, Molly?"

"I didn't come all the way up here to sleep with you, Doc . . . not for two hundred dollars . . . not for three times that much."

"Who and where?"

This time it was Molly who laughed. "I tell you that, Doc, an' what would you be needin' me for? Now, you interested?"

"What if I'm not, Molly my girl? What if I just tell you to go on back over the mountain?"

"Then that's exactly what I'll do. I meet a lot o' men in my profession. Hungry men, most of 'em. I'll find one that's hungry enough."

"But will you find 'im in time?"

"A third o' the take, Doc. That's not for dealin' about, so don't try."

Doc Henry poured them a drink. He downed his in a single gulp.

"You brought a dude with you. How's come?"

"He's not what I told Charlie he was. He's my contact with the Mexicans."

"What Mexicans, Molly?" Doc Henry turned surly. He hadn't stayed alive as long as this by being careless.

"Only one. You had a chance at him once but your men messed it up for you, didn't they?" Doc was caught off guard. "A girl, a woman and a young man."

"You whored with somebody, Molly. One o' my men. They opened up to you."

"Blarney! If you can't trust your own kind, Doc, I'm not wantin' to do business with you. But don't think you're the only one can make a fortune and a contact in these mountains. You're not!'"

"Yeah," Doc said, softly. "I'll deal with you Molly
. . . a third." He turned and pointed a finger at her.
"But I've got my own deal to make first."

Molly shrugged and said, "Fine. It'll take a bit to
set mine up anyway. Now I'll be askin' you to let my
man come and go as he needs to."

"Charlie Bojack rides with him . . . everywhere."

"No. If Butler rides in with a gunny on his back
there'll be trouble. He goes alone. I trust 'im and
you'll have to trust me." Doc grabbed Molly's arm,
up high. He nearly lifted her from her feet as he
pulled her close. The stubble of his beard scraped
across her cheeks and his breath was hot and reeked
of bad whisky. "You're hurtin' my arm," she said.

"It'll be a whole lot worse than that, Molly, if
you're lyin' to me. You think I won't put you under
same as anybody?"

"No, Doc . . . I don't think that."

"Then we'll deal, Molly, and you an' me, we'll
make it official tonight." The idea revolted her but
Molly knew she had pushed as far as she could.

6

Jim Buttrey had told Molly everything he knew. Morgan knew it now, and he didn't like it one damned bit. Unfortunately, there was nothing he could do about it. Molly had planned her vengeance even before Morgan entered the picture. Buttrey's death was only a small part of her motive. Doc Henry had also been responsible for the death of Molly's little sister. The outlaw didn't know that but Molly did, and Morgan knew she'd get Doc even at the cost of her own life.

"You've put a lot of people's lives in danger," Morgan told her, "just to kill Doc Henry."

"I'd as soon see 'im hang, Mahrgan, but I swear to you on me sister's grave, Doc Henry will die. I'll play along with you for now but if you don't get him, I will."

"The Mexicans? Is that legitimate?"

"To be sure, but I don't want him to get that far. I think he'll tell me what I need to know about his deal with the Apaches. Once he's done that, we can make a plan to stop him." Molly walked across the

46

room, stood quietly for a moment and then turned back to face Morgan. "I've told you everything," she said. "Now who are you workin' for and why? I know it's not all for the money."

"U.S. Senator Venable. Doc killed his youngest daughter, his son, and his wife. Emmy Venable is the girl I told you about . . . his other daughter. I'm working for him, officially. I'm a Pinkerton agent, same as Jim was."

"This Emmy woman can do us in," Molly said. "Can you control her?" Morgan mentally smiled to himself. Control Emmy Venable? It was laughable after the way she'd set him up. Morgan knew better than to let Molly in on that part.

"I can handle her," he replied.

"Sure you can, Mahrgan," Molly said, grinning, "but can you control her?" Molly didn't wait for an answer. She had a meeting with her girls. They would be instructed to elicit as much information out of Doc Henry's men as they could. Most were experts at it. While Molly was doing that, Morgan decided to play his hand. He'd simply go out into the open, ask to see Doc Henry personally. If there was anyone in camp who recognized him, he might as well get it over with fast.

Charlie Bojack ushered Morgan into Doc's house and then left. Doc was studying a map. Finally, he fired up a Cheroot and looked up. He eyed Morgan carefully.

"I seen you before, dude. That bothers me 'cause I don't recollect exactly where it was."

"Probably in Creede. Walsenburg maybe."

"Yeah . . . maybe. Maybe not. Anyways, when I finally recollect you'd better hope it was someplace right. Now dude, what Mexican do you work for?"

"Senor Valesquez. I am his aide."

"Can you speak for him—official, I mean?"

"I can."

"How's come? You're sure no Mex."

"I served with the American delegation for five years. He trusts me because I put him onto a source for weapons, women and other things he needed to support his revolution." Morgan was more than a little surprised at Doc Henry's grasp and knowledge of such matters. He suddenly realized he'd have to be on guard.

"So you know who his best field general is . . . don't you?"

"General Quesada? Of course." Morgan relaxed a little and made himself comfortable in a nearby stuffed chair. "You will not deal with him, however; you will deal with me and me only."

"And maybe when I'm through dealin' with you . . . I'll kill you, dude." Doc Henry smiled and his hand flashed to his hip.

"From all I've heard about you," Morgan replied, calmly, "I hardly think you'd risk a hundred thousand dollars just for the fun of putting a bullet in me." Doc's eyebrows raised and Morgan took advantage of the reaction. "Yes, Mister Henry . . . one hundred thousand. That's the sum I've been authorized to offer as payment for the rifles."

"In cash?"

"In silver, just as Miss O'Flynn told you."

"When and where?" Doc asked. Morgan chuckled. "You laughin' at me?"

"At your question. As you were told earlier, if you have that information, you have no need for my services or those of Miss O'Flynn, do you?"

"Okay, dude, what's next?"

"I will make contact with Senor Valesquez and tell him we have made a bargain. By the time you finish the job you have to do, the arrangements will be made." Morgan stood up and walked to the door. "Incidentally," he said, "just when will you be finished?"

"Ten days," came the reply. Morgan's nonchalance had paid off. "I'll want half the silver then and the balance on delivery."

Morgan turned around and said, "You'll have two thirds of the silver then and the rest on delivery. Miss O'Flynn wants her share up front as well." Morgan gave Doc Henry a little smile, a wave and walked out.

Charlie Bojack came back into the room, having entered the house from the rear. Doc looked up at him.

"You know that dude?"

"They's somethin' familiar about him," Charlie answered.

"Yeah . . . yeah there damned sure is, and I don't like it. Put a man on 'im, Charlie, a man what'll stick like flies to horse dung."

"Jake Trist just rode in. How 'bout him?"

"Good choice. If the dude is what he claims, Jake'll have no trouble findin' out. If he ain't," Doc continued, grinning, "Jake'll have no trouble killin' 'im."

Jake Trist was a quarter-breed Mescalero and one of the best trackers in the Southwest. He was also lightning fast with his guns. He wore two and was equally skilled with either hand. He'd ridden with

Quantrell, served as a deputy marshal for Wyatt Earp, and scouted for the army. Mostly, Jake Trist was a killer.

While Charlie Bojack was meeting with Jake, Molly sat down with her girl Gretchen, from South Fork. They thought they were alone. In fact, within earshot was the new girl who'd shown up in South Fork. Even now, no one knew anything about her but her first name. It was Elizabeth, but most just called her Beth.

Molly confided everything in Gretchen. She too had been a victim of Doc Henry and was seeking revenge. Gretchen was both surprised and relieved at the news about who Lee Morgan really was and why he was there. Beth was shocked. A few minutes after Molly and Gretchen separated, Beth slipped out of the room and made her way to the bunk houses used by Doc Henry's men. She singled one of them out, a young one. They left together, laughing.

Alone, hidden by a cluster of boulders, the young man finally spoke.

"What's this all about, Beth? I told you last night, I'm not leavin' and I'm not quittin' Doc Henry. This here is the only way I'll git enough money for us to live on and help Momma too."

"It's a trap, Billy . . . ever'thing is a trap. Miss Molly is in on it and that new man that come with her, that man named Butler. Well he's really a Pinkerton man an' his name is Lee Morgan. They plan to do somethin' to trap all o' you."

"Little sister, are you sure? Absolute sure?"

"I heard 'em, Billy. I heard Miss Molly and Gretchen talkin'. I'm sure, and if we don't light out o' here right now. Billy Frye, we'll both be daid."

Elizabeth Frye was only nineteen. She had been looking for her brother for more than a year, off and on. Billy had ridden away from their run-down little farm after his father died. He'd been sure he could earn enough to take care of the family of eight. He drifted for a few weeks, finally ending up in Creede. There, because of his way with horses, Billy fell in with the Halstead family. It was through Luke that he finally joined Doc Henry's gang. The money was easy, regular, and there was no law within a hundred miles.

When Beth's mother fell ill, she asked a neighbor for help and then went off in search of Billy. The trail finally led her to Molly O'Flynn's whore house. Now she was scared and shocked at the life in which she found Billy. Too, he'd taken to wearing a six gun and had even bragged to her about his skill with it. He was, in Beth's eyes, a gun fighter.

Billy escorted Beth back to the girl's quarters and reassured her that he would be safe. In fact, Billy wasn't exactly sure what he was going to do. He suffered no ill feelings about stealing army guns and selling them to the Apaches. But he had learned recently about the atrocities perpetrated by Doc Henry's men upon innocent victims. He'd already planned to do only one more job for Doc, collect what was due him, and ride out. Now he was facing the most difficult and dangerous decision of his young life.

While Billy struggled with his feelings, the safety of his sister and the knowledge she had shared with him, Lee Morgan rode out of the camp. He had been on the trail less than an hour before he knew he was being followed.

The discovery was no surprise to Morgan. Doc Henry was certainly not above a lie or a double-cross in any deal with anybody. Morgan's problem was simply one of keeping Jake Trist from finding out the truth. It seemed to him that the best way to do that would be to actually meet with the Mexican Ambassador. Morgan knew that he could gain such an appointment by merely using the Venable name. The Ambassador's men would deal with Jake Trist, and the situation would lend credibility to Molly's story. Ambassador Valesquez maintained an office in Farmington, New Mexico Territory. Morgan would telegraph his request and set up the meeting at the Chimney Rock Indian agency. It was about equal distance from Farmington and Creede.

Morgan spotted his pursuer more than once, but he made certain he wasn't seen. He had hoped to identify the man but the distance was too great. Finally, Morgan decided simply to ride on back to Creede and execute his plan. It was, he was satisfied, a good one. What he didn't and couldn't count on was Emmy Venable!

7

Morgan's timing couldn't have been better if he'd planned it. He rode hard and fast out of Winchester Valley and back to South Fork. The less time he spent in Creede now, the better. It was from South Fork that Morgan sent his telegraph to Senor Valesquez. That done, he found himself a room.

His arrival back in South Fork was timed almost exactly with that of Emmy Venable. She had managed to entice the Butterfield stage driver to return her to South Fork the very same day Morgan had chloroformed her. In the days that followed, she learned enough facts to formulate a plan of her own. It included sense enough to stay clear of Creede, which was where she believed Morgan to be. It was no small shock to her when she saw him enter the very rooming house where she was staying.

Emmy watched and waited. Morgan finally left his room and made his way to a room down the hall. It was equipped with a cattle tank that served as a bath tub. Morgan had a towel wrapped around him and his Colt in his hand. Emmy slipped into his room. Fifteen minutes passed. The door opened. Morgan closed it behind him, walked to the bed and slipped the Colt into its holster.

"Drop the towel," Emmy said. Morgan was half way between the bed and the chair which held his britches. He looked. She was leveling the sawed-off at him. "Don't get the idea I won't use it. I'm not that sure of anything right now, especially you." She motioned with the shotgun. Morgan looked down just a little sheepishly, then let the towel drop.

"You're a threat to this whole operation, Emmy," Morgan said. "That's why I bush-whacked you. Any one of Doc Henry's men could recognize you."

"I'm not stupid, Morgan, but I'm also not as full of blind trust as my father is." Emmy's eyes had really never left Morgan's groin. The idea that he was again being victimized by this woman somewhat angered Morgan, but the anger was tempered with his memory of the Windsor Hotel. Too, bedding her one more time would offer him his best chance to gain the upper hand. Emmy Venable had other ideas. "Lie down," she said. Morgan didn't hestitate. Even the minimal anticipation of her against him began to manifest itself and by the time he was on the bed, his cock was semi-rigid.

Emmy kept the shotgun pointed at him as she fumbled through her handbag. Morgan's eyes widened when she produced a pair of handcuffs. She threw them at him and said, "Cuff your wrists to the center post." Morgan's mouth started to move but Emmy pulled the hammers back on both shotgun barrels. Morgan complied. Emmy leaned the shotgun against the wall, removed all her clothing and used the drawstrings from her corset to secure

Morgan's ankles to the footboard.

She positioned herself over his chest and then leaned forward. Her breasts brushed his face, their hardened tips caressed his lips. She chuckled. She was enjoying the power as much as, maybe more than, the act itself. She reversed her body, eased her bottom directly over Morgan's face and then lowered it. "Lick it." The words weren't a feminine plea but a demand. "Do it until I say stop."

Lee Morgan wasn't accustomed to taking orders. Even this one stirred irritation deep within him. Partly, his mind conjured up flashing memories of the power he exerted over Molly O'Flynn. The tables were turned and the role was a new one. Those things aside, Morgan's expertise was in no way hindered.

Emmy increased her own pleasure with timed movements of her hips and settled lower so that she might savor every movement of Morgan's tongue. In just a minute or so, her hands found the softness of her own breasts and she kneaded the flesh and toyed with the nipples. Her eyes were glazed with passion and she licked her lips with every prod of Morgan's tongue.

She scooted back just a bit farther and then leaned forward onto her forearms. Her own mouth went to work now. She sucked and licked and caressed Morgan's blood-gorged shaft, his balls, inner thighs and lower abdomen. This too was new for Morgan, at least from Emmy Venable. She had made no such overtures while they were in Denver. She was an expert as well.

Emmy's whole body suddenly stiffened. She was on her hands and knees and her breathing sounded almost labored. Morgan couldn't see her face but her eyes were rolled back, her teeth clenched and sweat trickled down her cheeks onto her neck. She shuddered. A moment later, she eased herself off the bed, stood up, spread her legs and placed her hands on her hips.

"You are very good, Morgan . . . really. Thank you." Morgan reacted inside. He felt a gut wrenching tension. His balls ached and his cock twitched reflexively. Emmy's head went back slightly and she laughed.

"You've made your point," Morgan said. It was all he said. Anything else would probably sound like begging. That he didn't intend to do. Emmy sat on the edge of the bed. She thrust two fingers down between her legs and rubbed until they were shiny with her own juices of satisfaction. She rubbed them along Morgan's cock and then repeated the procedure, this time wetting his nipples. She leaned down and licked first one, then the other. She felt the muscles tighten, the breath sucked in. She raised up and laughed again. She studied Morgan's face, closely. His teeth were clenched but it was not from passion. He was determined to resist.

"You'd like to finish, wouldn't you?" Morgan didn't answer. Emmy stroked his cock again. It's head looked so swollen it appeared on the verge of bursting open. She stopped. "Well, wouldn't you?" Morgan nodded almost imperceptibly. Emmy laughed. "Not good enough, Morgan. Say it! Say," she lowered her tone slightly, "Emmy, I'd like to cum.' "

"Go to hell." She laughed and lowered her head to his chest. Her tongue flicked over his swollen nipples and her hand was pulling, slow, even strokes on his cock. Morgan felt all his own juices rushing to their release. He tensed and strained against his bonds. Emmy stopped. Morgan's breath stopped too. He tried to concentrate on completing his desire but her timing had been perfect.

"Say it, Morgan. Say the words," she paused, caressed his cock again and added, "and say 'Please, Emmy.' "

Lee Morgan had been around a lot of women, a lot of experienced women. Molly enjoyed her submissiveness and Morgan had bedded down with more than one who enjoyed a certain sexual dominance. Emmy was not like any of them. It was not the sexual satisfaction she enjoyed but the power she wielded. Suddenly, Morgan was feeling something else. A feeling with which he was a hundredfold more familiar. It was a feeling of danger. This woman, this seemingly innocent victim of her father's wealth and her family's fate, was dangerous. Sex was the bait but death was the trap. Morgan knew, suddenly and certainly, that Emmy Venable would use the shotgun.

"I'd like to . . . to cum, Emmy . . . *please!*" She laughed. She stood up, hovering over him for a moment, like the Black Widow just before it devours its male mate. She went to her bag and returned to the bed with the handcuff key. She undid the manacles and then hurriedly crossed the room, picked up the shotgun, turned back and levelled it at Morgan's head.

"Then please do so," she said. "I'd like to watch." Morgan hadn't masturbated since he was nine years old. He'd never done it in front of a woman. The order had a predictable effect. His cock softened somewhat. The reaction only made matters worse. "Looks like you'll have to play with it a little, doesn't it, Morgan?" She cocked the shotgun again. Morgan played. He stroked, trying hard to concentrate only on Emmy's naked and still inviting body. His eyes half closed and in a moment it was over. Sweat rolled from his muscular body and his face burned from a combination of involuntary embarrassment and increasing anger. It had all been done to a background of Emmy Venable's sinister laugh.

Morgan reached for the draw strings around his ankles. Emmy stopped him. "Just before you do that, you'd better understand one thing." Morgan looked at her. "I've got two men with me, good men. They know you but you've never seen them. If you have any ideas about getting rid of me again, I'd suggest you forget them."

"It's your neck," Morgan said. He freed himself and got dressed. Even watching Emmy dress, Morgan realized he'd probably never be aroused by her again. It wasn't what she had forced him to do but her own state of mind which bothered . . . even frightened him. Most of the men he faced were predictable. Their skills could be judged by their actions, the gun they wore and the way they wore it. Emmy Venable could not be so judged and Morgan wouldn't drop his guard again.

As Morgan figured it, he had nothing to lose by telling Emmy the entire plan. She wasn't about to go away and in this case, Morgan reckoned that what she didn't know could kill him. She listened, nodding occasionally. When he finished, Emmy spoke. Her voice was once again that of an innocent girl with vengeance in her heart.

"You know you were followed." Morgan nodded. "Do you know the man?"

"No. Haven't got that good a look at him yet."

"My men did. He's called Trist."

"Jake Trist! Shit! He's one of the best trackers in the country."

"And one of the fastest guns too, I've heard."

"Yeah, that too."

"Well he doesn't know about me . . . or my men. We can handle him."

"You do that and we'll all be in trouble. Stay put Emmy, and stay out of it . . . just for now. Let me meet the Mexican Ambassador and let his men handle Jake Trist."

"You mean trust you?"

"Yeah, Emmy, that's exactly what I mean."

Emmy was about to protest when a knock took her attention to the door and Morgan's to his Colt.

"Got an answer fer ya Mister Butler, from down in Farmin'ton." Morgan opened the door just far enough to accept the telegraph message and hand the messenger a dollar. "Thanky, Mister Butler, thanky." Morgan unfolded the paper and read its contents aloud.

"The Ambassador regrets to inform you that he will be unable to meet with you at this time due to the press of affairs in our country. He will contact Senator Venable when his schedule permits such an appointment." Morgan looked at Emmy and frowned.

"What now?"

"I ride to Chimney Rock same as before. We know

the facts, but Jake Trist doesn't."

"He'll find out when he gets there."

"Not if you stay here and send a message down ahead of me. I'll make certain he gets that one. I'll just fake one to confirm the gun purchase and the amount, with regrets that the Ambassador couldn't meet me in person."

"How do you know somebody else isn't following you?"

"Because I know Jake Trist, at least by reputation. He doesn't need any help."

"I don't like this, Morgan, not any of it."

"You don't have to like it, Emmy, just do it." She hesitated a moment and then nodded. The reaction still surprised Morgan. How suddenly demure and obedient Emmy seemed. It was, he concluded, all the more reason to be cautious.

If Ambassador Valesquez's message was a minor setback in Morgan's plans, a major one was even then riding into the Chimney Rock stage station. The lone rider, sinister in appearance, dismounted and paused after pushing the bat wing doors open. His eyes adjusted quickly to the dim light. He satisfied himself that there was no danger. He walked over to the long bar.

"A whisky."

"Just got some ice in, mister, if'n you'd be wantin' a cold beer."

"I said whisky." The bartender shrugged, noting the long, deep scar on the man's right cheek. That was the only feature which distinguished Johnny Jared from his brother Doc Henry. "When's the next stage for Creede?"

"Tomorrow noon, if'n it don't git way-layed."

"I need a room."

"Upstairs, mister. Two dollars with a bath."

"I just want it for sleeping."

"Dollar, then. Clean linen but no towels."

Over the years it had been Doc Henry Jared whose name and occasional likeness appeared on lawmen's *dodgers*. There were many stories, however, about just which of the Jared boys was the fastest. Ironically, one of the stories focused on Johnny Jared being shot in the leg by a man who, so said the witnesses, was the fastest they'd ever seen. As the story was told and re-told, the identification of the man with the fast gun came into it. Now it was generally accepted that it had been Buckskin Frank Leslie. Few people knew that Frank had fathered a son. Among those who didn't know was Johnny Jared. What he did know was what the man who'd bested him looked like. He really didn't care about the man's name.

Jared retired early that evening. It was unusually quiet in Chimney Rock and Jared felt at ease with himself. He'd returned to the territory at the request of his brother and he'd done the job that had been asked of him. He rode into Durango, staked himself to adequate supplies and then rode into New Mexico territory. He rode down to Chaco creek and there met and made a deal with a Jicarilla Apache renegade named Naschitti. In just ten more days, Johnny and Doc Henry would deliver twenty cases of army rifles and ammunition to Nashitti. In return, Naschitti's warriors were to raid an army pay wagon as it journeyed from Farmington to Durango. They would net about $50,000 for their efforts and were obliged to give only a thousand apiece to Doc Henry's men. They'd split the rest and be done with the Apaches at the same time.

It was nearer to two o'clock than noon the next day before Johnny Jared finally boarded the Butterfield stage for Creede. It was a full load. Two saloon girls, a drummer, an army sergeant, a young lawyer and Jared. There was no money aboard so there was no shotgun rider. The driver was a craggy-faced old freight skinner and knew every rock, bump and bend in the trail. By suppertime, they'd reached Pagosa Springs. The run, well into the evening, would finally end at Wolf Creek Station. It was on the western slope of Wolf Creek Pass, nearly 11,000 feet of pure hell. It was a climb not even the best skinners would try at night. On the eastern side of the mountain was another stage stop where, by mid-afternoon, the stage would stop and change stock.

Bearing down on that station, as Johnny Jared dozed off and on in the stage coach headed toward him, was Lee Morgan. A couple of miles behind him rode Jake Trist. Unknown to either of them, Trist had his own shadow. At Molly O'Flynn's order, her man Trigg was not far behind. The tiny stage stop might also become a permanent rest stop for any one of them.

8

It was summertime but the air smelled of fall. It was cool, crisp and clean. It poured down from the San Juans and carried with it the scent of pine and the sound of rustling Aspen. Morgan stepped outside the small stage depot, took in a deep breath and let his eyes scan the terrain around him. He was still attired in his dude clothes but the Bisley was now in place. He felt secure again.

The station agent stepped out behind him and eyed the sky. It was cloudless. " 'Nother mighty purty day in the makin.' "

"Yeah," Morgan agreed.

"You ridin' on west, mister, or waitin' fer the Butterfield?"

"I'll be moving on. I'd like to get to Pagosa Springs by dark."

"You'll be pushin' that roan o' your'n, mister. You ever clumb the pass?" Lee shook his head. "Well, 'tain't like most of 'em. Got a mean streak. Turn on ya real sudden. Rock slides, snow and ice bustin' loose," the agent paused and looked toward the summit, "varmints too. Makes even the best o' horses skitterish. They's the bones o' horse and man alike . . . some say a foot deep . . . at the bottom o' one o' the drops."

"You know another way into the Springs from here?"

"Nope."

"Then I guess I'll have to chance it." Lee smiled at the agent, in part about the tall tales. "I'd best get to it." Lee slapped the man on the shoulder and headed for the stable.

Morgan was about two-thirds of the way toward the summit when he was forced to dismount. The agent had been right about the rock slides. Half the narrow trail was blocked and the outside edge of it looked none too safe. He began to clear some of the smaller rocks away but he doubted there'd be room for the stage to pass. He decided to wave it down when he finally met it and warned the driver.

The stage itself was already at the summit but not without its own problems. A hub had snapped and it had lost a wheel. The male passengers were helping the driver to get set for repairs, and Johnny Jared was chopping down a small pine to assist them in raising the rear of the coach when the time came.

"Fella ridin' our way," the drummer said, pointing. Everyone stopped their work and looked up. Jared was still working on the tree, about fifty yards away. "Howdy, mister. S'pose you could spare us a hand?"

"Yeah," Morgan replied, dismounting. "You got more troubles about half way down. Rock slide. I cleared some of it but you'll have to lever a couple of big boulders out of the way." Morgan looked over the passengers carefully, studied the heavy coach's position and then turned back for a last glance at the trail he'd just come over. Somewhere behind him, he knew Jake Trist was still coming.

"Hey, you at the coach . . . give me a hand with this log." Morgan was surprised. The voice came from the opposite side of the stage . . . a man's voice. Another passenger. He was tense with a sudden alertness.

"Had a fella choppin' down a pine to use fer some leverage," the driver said. Morgan nodded and started around the coach.

Johnny Jared was bent over at the waist, wrestling the log loose from between two rocks. The stage driver, the army sergeant and Morgan, who was out front, were headed toward him.

"Hang on, mister, and we'll give ya a hand," the driver hollered. Jared straightened and turned. His eyes met Morgan's. Both men squinted. Morgan's features seemed to leap from his face and reform themselves in Jared's mind. A voice. A threat. A flashing Colt. Jared's mind recalled the grunt he'd heard and the searing pain in his right knee.

"Jeezus! Lee Morgan!"

Morgan's own thoughts had been hurtling through his head with the speed of bullets . . . but he had that all-important edge. This time, it was his recent visit with Doc Henry. Even as Jared's mind was recreating their last meeting, Morgan's right hand was in motion. A split second had passed. Jared's fingers tightened around the butt of the gun strapped to his left leg. Morgan's peripheral vision registered the movement of a man's body off to his left. The stage driver was diving for the ground. The army sergeant stood, petrified by the scene unfolding a few feet from him.

The Bisley's barrel belched out blue smoke and the crack of shot bounced against the rocky surroundings, echoing down the slopes of Wolf Creek Pass. Morgan had shot to kill. The sergeant's eyes had blinked and he'd missed the draw. The bullet struck home . . . Johnny Jared's heart . . . dead center. His own gun barked and the bullet ripped through Morgan's pant leg about boot high, tearing away the boot's pull strap. Jared blinked. He coughed. Blood filled the cavity that was his open mouth. His left hand jerked, reflexively, and he fell, face down.

Morgan whirled. "Stand fast," he ordered. No one moved. His brain sent him another warning. The shot! Jake Trist must have heard it. He'd want to know about it.

"I saw it all, mister, ever' move," the army sergeant said, "the man pulled on ya. It was self defense fer sure."

Jake Trist pulled back hard on the reins. A shot! Two! They were from different guns. He jerked his rifle free from its boot, tucked it under his arm and spurred his mount. He crouched low and dug the spurs deeper still into the big animal's flanks. He could see the figures of two men near the coach. A third was on his hands and knees, trying to get up. Trist's eyes scanned ahead of him. Another man was face down, not moving. He saw a horse nearby and recognized the animal. He'd seen it, recently . . . Durango! It was Johnny Jared's horse.

"Look out!" It was the sergeant. They were his

last words. The Henry repeater barked once and a small, red spot appeared on the sergeant's forehead. Morgan dropped to one knee, swung his right arm in a leading movement and squeezed the trigger. The shot lifted Jake's hat from his head. Morgan rolled. The Henry barked again and Morgan heard the shell splintering the wood of the coach door.

Lee Morgan came to his feet, still crouching. His eyes flashed back and forth over the short distance the horse had traveled, but the animal was riderless. Jake Trist had leaped from its back, dug in his heels to control his forward momentum, spun around, and dropped behind a tree stump.

Morgan's right arm moved forward about two inches. The Colt was waist high. He squeezed the trigger. The shot was deafening ... too much noise for a Colt. One final, ear-shattering *craaack* echoed through the rocks. Lee's eyes caught the shiny movement of the Henry's barrel. Its bullet struck, digging up the dirt twenty feet in front of Lee's position. The Colt's bullet struck Jake Trist right between the eyes, but only because his body had been lifted up by the force of a missile from a .50 calibre Sharps. That bullet had caught Jake in the side, just below his rib cage.

Now there was silence, a macabre stillness. A twig snapped and Morgan's body turned, tense, the Colt ready again. He saw Molly's man, Trigg, riding slowly toward the coach, a Sharps cradled on his free arm.

"I don't like my trail being dogged, not even by friends," Morgan said. There was no answer. "Shit!" Morgan remembered—Trigg was a mute. The tall man dismounted, slipped the Sharps back into its scabbard and walked over to Morgan. He extended his hand. Morgan stared at him. Trigg was half smiling. Morgan shook his head, and then shook Trigg's hand.

Morgan had plenty of problems and he knew it. He might get away with an explanation about Jake Trist's death, but he dared not mention Doc Henry's brother, and there would be plenty of questions about the sergeant. And no matter what he said, he knew no one on that stage coach would keep their mouths shut. On top of that, the Chimney Rock station had just been equipped with a telegraph.

By the time they'd reached South Fork again, a cavalry patrol was waiting.

"Everyone inside." The two women left the coach first and Morgan could see who was barking the order. A leathery-faced old sergeant-major. He assisted the women, half smiling, and then wrinkled his brow as the men emerged. Trigg and Morgan climbed up and aided two troopers in lowering the trio of bodies to the ground. That done, they joined the others inside. The driver had already given his account of the activities and so had the women.

A young lieutenant with a shock of blonde, touseled hair and pink cheeks confronted Morgan and Trigg.

"Lieutenant Tyson Yates, U.S. Fifth Cavalry, sir. I have been charged with determining the cause or causes and the party or parties responsible for the death of Sergeant Henry Willis."

"Only one cause, only one party, lieutenant," Morgan said. "Man named Jake Trist fired a rifle at me, missed and hit the sergeant instead."

"And the reason for the attack?"

"I figure Trist and his companions were planning a holdup. The busted wheel messed up their schedule and this fella," Morgan continued, pointing at Trigg, "just happened along."

"Is that right?" The lieutenant addressed himself to Trigg. Trigg nodded. "Your name, sir?"

"He can't tell you lieutenant. He's a mute."

The lieutenant frowned, rubbed his chin in a nervous gesture and then said, "Then your name, sir?"

"Butler. Wilfrid Butler."

"And your line of business?"

"I'm a gambler . . . mostly."

"By the accounts I heard a few minutes ago . . . Mister Butler, it would seem you're a mighty handy man with a gun."

"It was self defense, lieutenant. We caught them by surprise and came out on top. I don't know anywhere that has a law against that."

"Nor do I, sir, if that's what happened." The lieutenant turned to the others. "You are all under army detention over night. Let's hope we can clear this up by tomorrow, in which case you will be free to go." He turned back to Morgan. "I am requesting that you and your mute companion accompany me."

"Are we being arrested?"

"No, sir, but there are some additional questions."

The army had taken over a run-down hotel at the far end of town. It was there the lieutenant took Morgan and Trigg. Inside, they were asked to wait in what had once been a small dining room. After a few minutes, they were joined by the lieutenant and a captain who introduced himself as Phillip

Torrance.

"I haven't a great deal of time," he began, "and even less patience. I want the truth and I want it now. If I do not get it, gentlemen, then I will execute my rights and declare this community and those in it under martial law."

"Since when does the army take such a direct interest in territorial law?"

"A sergeant was killed. Perhaps you've forgotten."

"Not at all, captain, but there were several witnesses to the incident and they all told your lieutenant the same story." Morgan sat down, leaned back and half smiled. "Or have you forgotten, captain?"

"I'm looking for a gang of gun-runners. Sergeant Willis was enroute from Durango with information about one of them. I have reason to believe that the entire affair at Wolf Creek station was deliberately staged to eliminate him."

"At the cost of two innocent men?"

"This gang, mister, uh . . . Butler, wasn't it?" Morgan nodded. "This gang wouldn't hesitate to eliminate everyone on that stage if they felt threatened."

"And we're your best bet right now, right?"

"You are!"

Morgan carefully removed a letter from his pocket and handed it to the captain. It was his confirmation as a Pinkerton operative and bore the signature of Senator Venable. The captain read it twice and then looked up.

"How do I know you didn't lift this from one of the dead men?"

"Because I can tell you who they were as well. One of them was no doubt the very man your sergeant was looking for."

"And who might that be?"

"John Jared, the brother of the gang's leader, Doc Henry Jared."

"And the other man?"

"Jake Trist."

"Mister Morgan," the captain said, handing Lee the letter, "I'm going to verify what you tell me and I'm going to ask you to remain in town until tomorrow. You and your mute friend." Morgan pondered his position for a moment, even considering a quick verification by Emmy—but, somehow, he didn't feel comfortable with the choice. He simply nodded. "There are quarters here, not fancy, but I'm sure you've suffered worse."

"No doubt I have," Morgan said.

Sore-ass tired, Morgan slept fitfully that night. Half a dozen times he woke up, each time with a knot of discomfort deep in his belly. A good plan had gone sour and he couldn't be sure that Doc Henry didn't already know it. Molly and her girls could all be dead by now. He was glad when morning came.

It was near seven thirty before the captain finally asked Morgan and Trigg to meet with him. Morgan thought he looked grim. He soon found out why.

"I've substantiated your story, Mister Morgan, and I was told to give you your head."

"And you don't like that, do you, captain?"

"I not only don't like it, sir, I don't intend to abide by it. I don't take my orders from United States Senators. I stayed out of this situation when the last Pinkerton man showed up."

"Jim Buttrey?"

"I believe that was his name, yes. I won't make the same mistake again. I intend to stop these men before they supply those guns to Naschitti."

"I'm on the inside right now, captain, and so are several of my friends. If you go off on a half baked raid, they'll all get killed."

"And if I let you handle it and you fail, a lot more people will get killed. No, Mister Morgan, not this time. I'll work with you, but not for you."

Morgan was as tied up right now as he had been when Emmy Venable had him hand-cuffed to the bed. He didn't like being tied up at all, and this time there wasn't even any pleasure in it.

"What have you got in mind?" Morgan asked.

"An ambush. You and your friends set it up. I don't care how, but I do care where." The captain walked to a nearby desk and unfolded a map of the territory. Morgan joined in. "I know that Henry Jared is somewhere in the Uncompahgre Valley. I know it would be suicidal to attempt to take him on his own ground. You bring him out, Morgan; I'll do the rest." The captain pointed to a spot on the map. "Here, along the San Juan river, is an old mission called Gato. It's nestled in the closed end of a box canyon. Get him there and I'll do the rest."

"Sounds simple enough," Morgan said, "but just how the hell am I supposed to convince him to ride in there? Doc Henry hasn't stayed alive all these years by being stupid."

"Guns," the captain said, smiling, "lots and lots of guns. Among them, for bait, two Napoleon guns and one Gatling. It's a lot more than he expected."

"And because it's a lot more, Doc Henry will smell a skunk."

"Not if he has government confirmation and a personal request to deal on those guns only from the renegade Naschitti."

Morgan frowned. He looked Captain Torrance square in the eye. "The official confirmation I can understand, Captain, but how do you propose to get Naschitti's cooperation?"

"I have something the Apache wants perhaps even more than the guns." The captain smiled wryly. "I have Naschitti's son!"

9

"*Sumbitch!*" Doc Henry downed another shot of whisky and got up from behind his desk. "You're smarter'n ya look, dude." He winked at Molly. "This here pimp o' yours brought us back a fortune. Them Mexicans wanna deal an' we got more'n we figured on from the army to sell to Naschitti." Doc's Colt was suddenly levelled at Morgan's belly. " 'Less'n you're lyin' to me." He was grinning but Morgan knew he was still questioning such a lucrative proposition. Morgan decided to play his Ace.

"The deal is made, Jared, but it didn't come for you, Doc."

"Whatta you mean?"

"You were told not to have me followed. That was your first mistake. Senor Valesquez's men didn't take to Mister Trist."

"Jake?" Doc's eyes widened.

"He's dead, Jared. And so is your brother, Johnny."

The Colt's barrel caught Morgan a glancing blow, high up on his right cheek. His head snapped and a razor thin line of blood appeared.

"You're a lyin' sumbitch, Butler."

"You think I'd tell you that kind of news if it wasn't true?" Morgan wiped his cheek and feigned a dizziness he didn't feel. "Why risk my life for nothing?" Molly got to her feet and stood between the two men. Doc Henry was glowering but the look was slowly turning to shock.

"How?" Jared asked, weakly.

"I only know what I heard. Two men, Pinkerton agents, I heard, they ambushed your brother on the trail between Durango and Chimney Rock."

"Charlie! Get your ass in here . . . now!" Doc Henry screamed the order, downed three huge gulps of straight rye and hurled the empty bottle toward the door. It shattered just over Charlie Bojack's head. "You git on down to Creede. You find out about Jake and Johnny. You find out if this dude is tellin' me gospel. Soon as you do, you git on back."

Charlie Bojack eyed Morgan carefully. Morgan could tell he was still trying to recall where he'd seen him before. Eventually, he'd remember. Morgan didn't. Maybe it was a poster, maybe a poker game, maybe even a shoot-out. It made little difference. Morgan remained calm. When he spoke, it was softly.

"You'll lose too much time with that, Jared. The deals are made. If they don't come down on schedule, they won't come down at all."

"You tellin' me my business, dude?"

"I'm telling you mine. You do whatever you want with the Apache, but if you're not at the meeting place with Senor Valesquez on schedule there won't be any hundred thousand in silver."

"Maybe you should be givin' up on the Indian," Molly said, smiling. "Just take the deal I've made for you Doc."

"Pass up Naschitti? You are tryin' to set me up. I double cross him an' there'd be hell to pay, Molly girl." He turned back to Charlie Bojack. "Tell the men we'll ride out day after tomorrow. Follow the usual procedure. I don't want anybody stumblin' into Winchester Valley."

"I know you don't like changes," Morgan said, half smiling now and displaying some nervousness, "but after all, your brother did give his life for the deal. It's just a stroke of luck that I stumbled into it when I did."

"Yeah," Doc Henry said, "it was a lucky break. Now we'll find out if it was good luck or bad luck for you . . . dude!"

As Molly and Morgan left, young Billy Frye brushed by them on the way in. He stared at Morgan, hard. Inside, he cleared his throat, hefted his gun to display his newfound bravado and started to speak.

"Well, if'n it ain't little Billy Frye." Doc Henry uncorked another bottle, took a long drink from it and then handed it to Billy. "Wet your whistle, boy. You look like you need it." Billy nodded and complied. He nearly choked on the rotgut. Doc Henry laughed. "You git one o' them girls yet?"

"Uh . . . well no, boss, not yet."

"Well you'd best do it quick, boy. We're pullin' out day after tomorrow. Hell, what's the matter with you? Your dick rot and fall off? Why when I was your age, I'da had 'em all fucked by now . . . oncest anyways." He laughed again and took another drink.

"Boss . . . I . . . I come to . . . talk to you about somethin' important."

"That right? Well Billy boy, just you talk away. Few more days an' you'll be so damned rich you won't even want to talk to me. You can buy yourself as many fancy women as you want. Not whores like these but fancy, N'Orleans women. Besides, these here'll all be pushin' up daisies."

Billy frowned. "What?"

"Daisies, boy. Sod. Dead, Billy boy, cold, stone *dead.* Ever'one of 'em 'cept fer Molly."

"I . . . I don't understand, Mister Jared."

"Simple, boy. They seen too much an' they know too much." Doc Henry walked over, wrapped his arm around Billy's neck and half dragged him across the room. "You'll learn aplenty ridin' with me, boy, but if you don't learn nothin' else you'll learn not to trust nobody but your own kind." He slapped Billy on the back, laughed and then added, "An' only trust them when you can see 'em."

"Yes sir."

"Now what was it you wanted to tell me that was so all fired important?"

"Uh . . . well I was wonderin' if you thought I was ready to ride with you on the next job."

Doc Henry looked into Billy's eyes. The request puzzled him. It didn't seem to match Billy's concern when he first walked in. If Doc Henry Jared was short on anything, it wasn't his judgment of men.

"That's it?"

"Uh . . . yeah, boss."

"Bullshit!"

"Well . . . I was hopin' you'd let me ride as a gun

an' not just a lookout or watchin' the horses."

"A gun? So you think you've got that good, eh?"

"I've been practicinjg near ever' day now."

"You as good as Charlie here?"

"Well, I . . . I don't know."

"Then let's find out." Doc Henry jammed his hand into his pants pocket and pulled out a coin. "Draw when it hits the floor." He tossed it up. Billy's eyes were still on Doc. Suddenly they went up. At the same moment, the coin struck the wooden floor and bounced. Billy reached, but he was already staring into the barrel of Charlie Bojack's .45.

"I . . . I wasn't ready."

"That's right, boy, you wasn't an' you'd be dead. An' if'n you was ridin' with me, you'd have somebody else to keep an eye on and they'd be dead too. I'll tell you when you're ready, boy . . . me, not you." Billy nodded and eased toward the door.

Outside he took a deep breath of air and tried to settle his nerves. He'd had two close calls and he was more confused than ever. Doc was going to kill all those women. Maybe even Molly and for sure he'd kill Lee Morgan. Beth might talk too, if she thought Billy was in danger. He didn't know what to do.

Alone with Molly for the first time since his return, Morgan filled her in on the events which had transpired. By the time he was through, Molly was pacing and cursing under her breath. Suddenly, she stopped.

"You know, don't you, that Jared won't take every man he's got to meet Naschitti. Hell, Mahrgan, men been ridin' in here, steady, since you left. There must be thirty or more by now."

"Yeah I figured that."

"If the army even gets half of 'em they'll be lucky."

"Yeah . . . I figured that too."

"Damn you, Mahrgan! How can you be so bloody calm about it?"

"I took a little extra precaution, Molly. I telegraphed Senator Venable and asked him to see to it that there were some minor changes made in that gun shipment."

"Like what?"

"Like only one in five crates of rifles will actually contain rifles, and the shipment will be in that canyon two days ahead of schedule. The wagons bringing the shipment in will bypass the army and go direct to Gato mission."

"Can you be sure o' that, Mahrgan?" He handed her a dispatch. It was Senator Venable's reply to the request. "So you've done that much. How do you get the word to the Apache?"

"Your man Trigg handled that for me. Seems he has an Indian friend." Molly looked puzzled for a moment and then smiled. Trigg had been bedding down with an Apache maiden.

"I told you Trigg was a good man." Morgan nodded his agreement. "There's still Doc Henry. How do you convince him?"

"I'll handle that when we get to Creede. Remember, Doc Henry thinks I'm a man with all the right connections. I'll convince him of it by a simple visit to the good Captain."

Almost as though she'd been struck a blow, the whole scheme suddenly revealed itself to Molly.

"God A'mighty Mahrgan! You plan on runnin' half o' Doc's men into that canyon so's Naschitti can open them crates and find out he's been duped."

"That's about the size of it, Molly. By my reckoning, he'll be one mad Apache."

"An' we'll be rid o' half our worries."

"And the army should be able to take care of the other half. Captain Torrance commands three cavalry companies, that should be enough."

"And when he finds out he's been duped too . . . an' missed a chance to get Naschitti?"

"That, Molly, is Senator Venable's problem."

"The girl, Mahrgan . . . the Senator's daughter. What of her?" It was the only question Molly had asked for which Morgan had no answer. He still felt uneasy about her and he knew she wouldn't simply be sitting idly by.

"It's the only hand we've got, Molly . . . and she's the draw card."

"So it is, Mahrgan, so it is. I just hope it works." Morgan smiled. "There's an old Irish saying that covers it if it doesn't, Molly. I think it goes something like . . . I hope you're in heaven half an hour before the devil knows you're dead." Molly nodded but she wasn't smiling.

Throughout the next day, Morgan, Molly and her girls watched men ride into Winchester Valley. By nightfall they estimated Doc's gang had swelled to more than 60. Many of the girls spent time with Doc's top hands, mostly trying to keep them half drunk. One, however, stayed out of sight. Beth Frye was scared out of her wits and she hadn't spoken to Billy since the day she told him what she'd overheard. She was crying to herself when Gretchen walked in on her.

"What is it, Beth, what's wrong?" Beth shook her head but continued crying. Gretchen tried a second time. Still Beth resisted. "Did one of these jackasses hurt you?" Beth shook her head. Gretchen sat beside her and put an arm around her shoulder. "You're not the girl you claim to be, are you?" Now Beth looked up. Her eyes were wide and her expression gave Gretchen all the answer she needed.

"I lied to you," Beth blurted out. "I lied so I could get up here and help my . . . my . . ."

"Your what?"

"My brother." Beth confessed all to Gretchen, finally calming down enough to express her more immediate concerns. "I don't know if Billy's told anybody yet."

"I think we're safe in figuring he didn't," Gretchen replied. "We're all still alive." Gretchen stood up, walked a few feet and turned back. "You go fetch Billy right now. Get him back here."

"What do I say to him?"

"I don't give a damn what you say, Beth. Just get him here."

Gretchen watched Beth cross the compound and then hurried off to find Molly and Morgan. Just her tone, when she found them, was enough to get them to return to her quarters. She hastily informed them of Beth's real reason for being there. She had barely finished when Beth and Billy walked in. Billy saw Morgan and reached for his gun.

"You go ahead and kill me," Morgan said, "and then hope you can keep Doc Henry from killing you . . . and your sister." Billy holstered his gun.

"Have you told Doc Henry the truth?" Molly asked.

"I went to do it yesterday."

"But you didn't. Why not?"

"He's gonna kill ever'body, Mister Morgan. Ever'body but Molly. That's what he tol' me." Billy shook his head and looked, helplessly, at Beth. "Jeezus! What have I done?"

"The right thing," Molly offered. She looked at Morgan. "The thought had crossed my mind. I lost five girls up here once before. Doc Henry paid me well but he tol' me the Apache got 'em."

"Yeah, Molly, but the Apache wouldn't have killed them until they'd had their fun."

"I know that now."

"What do we do?" Billy asked.

"Just as you're told," Morgan said. "When, where, and how."

"Beth . . . what about her? One o' Doc's men has already talked about havin' her?"

"I'll handle that end," Molly said. "I'll tell Doc that one o' the Mexicans asked for a young girl . . . a new, nice young girl. I'll pick Beth. He won't argue about it."

"An' what do I do for now . . . anythin'?"

"Yeah, Billy," Morgan said, "keep your ears open and your mouth shut." He eyed the boy's rig. "Can you use that thing?"

"I can, yes sir. I been practicin' near ever' day now."

"I mean, can you kill a man with it?"

"I . . . I think so."

"You'd better decide, Billy, and fast. One of them will kill you while you're thinking."

A few of the newly arrived gang members had planned a little party with the girls that night. Gretchen promised to keep an eye on Beth. They all knew that some of those men would even ignore Doc Henry's orders if they got too drunk. Billy returned to his quarters, scared but feeling better. Molly sat quietly for several minutes, got up and walked to the door, and then turned back.

"I think I'll add just a wee bit o' spice to the pie."

"How's that?"

"A little double-cross talk to Doc. I'll let him think I don't give a damn about anybody but him an' me. A little larger share for both of us if you're out o' the way." Morgan pondered the idea for a moment and then nodded.

"Can't hurt a thing," he said. "It's Doc's kind of thinking."

"One thing does bother me, Mahrgan. Me girls. I don't want 'em gettin' hurt . . . or worse."

"Don't worry. Doc won't risk doing anything until both deals are over."

"He wants me to show 'im where those wagons with the Winchesters are comin' in."

"Do it. I'm supposed to talk to him too, in the morning. I'll remind him that Senor Valesquez will be expecting both of us. You and me."

"I'm prayin' you got this all figured right, Mahrgan." Molly walked out. Morgan watched her.

"So am I," he said to himself. "So am I, Molly girl."

10

The thunder of hoof beats jarred Morgan from his sleep. It was still dark outside, but he could see the silhouettes of the riders as they galloped by. Doc had moved the schedule ahead. Morgan was witnessing the departure of thirty-three of Doc's gang. They would ride to Gato mission and make the deal with Naschitti. The gang included four of his top guns, one of them a half-breed Apache named Brazo.

Morgan dressed hurriedly and made his way to Doc's house. He found Doc in an unusually jovial mood which Morgan attributed partly to Molly's double-cross talk of the day before.

"I made a couple o' changes, dude. I figure there's just enough time to make sure the deal with Naschitti comes off before we have to ride out and meet with the Mexican boys." He looked for a reaction.

"Smart move," Morgan said.

"An' I'm having Charlie Bojack lead the raid on them Winchesters. Me, Molly, an' a couple o' my

boys will ride with you, dude . . . back to Creede.
That way, we'll all be there together when everything gits confirmed." Morgan didn't like that, but
he couldn't afford to tip his hand.

"Another good move, Doc. Now I understand why
you've stayed alive so long." Doc liked the
compliment. He grinned and then pulled Morgan to
a nearby map.

"You pick the spot fer that raid on them Winchesters?"

"Yeah. Anything wrong with it?"

"Not if'n you're levelin' with me, no. If not, it'd
sure be a good spot fer an ambush. You'd best remember I'll be watchin' ya, dude . . . real close like."

The ride to Creede seemed to take forever, and
Molly was visibly nervous. Doc picked up on it and
Morgan knew it. Doc's two gunnies rode behind him
all the way. Nonetheless, Morgan's luck was
holding. He managed the phony dispatch
confirming a time and place for their meeting with
Senor Valesquez. Doc was impressed.

"A hunnert thousand in silver," he said. He
looked up and laughed. "Sure beats holdin' up them
Butterfields, wouldn't ya say, Molly?"

"It does that, Doc, surely it does."

"Now, dude . . . part two. You git on down to that
Army cap'n an' bring me back the word that ever'
thing is still okay with Naschitti. Army's not
supposed to meet up with them guns fer three more
days, that right?"

"Right," Morgan said. "But tomorrow, your boys
will have already ridden into Gato and made the
deal."

"Well, I'd still like to make sure. An' I'd like to see you walk into that army office."

"Let's go."

"Jess here'll do it." Doc looked up at the big, scar-faced man who stood near the door. He was cradling a scatter gun on one arm. "Watch 'im, Jess . . . watch 'im close."

The army's small office in Creede was at the far end of town. Morgan stayed to the back alley until he reached the main street. There was little activity there and he hurried across, cast a brief glance back at his unwanted shadow and entered the office. His luck was still holding, but he'd just walked into a hornet's nest.

Inside, he found himself facing a pink-cheeked private.

"I'm here to see Captain Torrance." The boy looked up, a quizzical expression on his face.

"I beg your pardon, sir."

"Captain Torrance . . . your commanding officer. Tell him Mister Morgan is here to see him."

The boy frowned and stood up. "Sir . . . you must have been out of town."

"Yeah, but what the hell does that have to do with anything?"

"Sir . . . Captain Torrance died four days ago. The Fifth cavalry troops stationed here are now under the command of Brevet Lieutenant-Colonel Yates."

"Jeezus," Morgan mumbled. He took his hat off, rubbed his forehead and glanced back at the window. He could see Doc's man eyeing the office. "Yates then, where is he?"

"In the field, sir. Acting on his own responsibility, Lieutenant-Colonel Yates took two companies south to hunt down and arrest . . . or kill . . . the renegade Apache, Naschitti.''

"Shit! When?''

"Two days ago, sir. He took the action following a raid of hostiles on our stockade. During that raid, we lost a half a dozen men and our prisoner . . . Naschitti's son.''

"The crazy sonuvabitch,'' Morgan mumbled. He put his hat on, quickly forced a most uneasy composure and walked out. He had cleared about half the distance between the office and where Doc's man, Jess, was standing when someone called out to him.

"Right there, Morgan . . . that's far enough.'' Morgan looked at Jess, dived for the cover of a horse trough and yelled at the same moment.

"Pinkerton men!'' The reaction was predictable. Jess cut loose with both barrels of the scatter-gun. There was a howl. By then, Morgan had the Bisley working. There had been three targents. The shotgun took out the middle one, the biggest. It ripped open his whole belly. Morgan recognized Luke Halstead. His own shots dropped the other two.

The sudden appearance of the trio, Morgan's swift action and Jess's reaction were closely followed by stark reality. Jess suddenly realized the name which had been called out. He'd heard the sharp crack of the .45 . . . a weapon the dude wasn't supposed to be carrying. Now he found himself staring into it. He reached but it was too late. Jess took the shot high in the chest.

The melee had brought the pink-cheeked army trooper and a couple of his companions into the street. Morgan's options were slim to none.

"Get one of your men out of here and find Yates. Tell him Creede is threatened." Morgan rushed over to the young trooper and held his Pinkerton letter in the boy's face. "Get word to whoever is in charge of the reserve company to get those men *off* and *on*. Tell them to ride to where the Rio Grande cuts the trail to Wagon Wheel Gap south of here. Don't argue, don't ask questions, just do it. Now, trooper."

"Yes, sir!"

Morgan double-timed it back to Molly's place, once again through the back alley. He couldn't figure who tipped Luke Halstead to his presence in town or, in fact, how Luke had learned who he was. All he did know what that Doc Henry would have heard the shots.

The shots had drawn many of Molly's men out of her place by the front way. The commotion was what Morgan was counting on to distract Doc long enough to give him a plausible account of the affair. It didn't work.

The shotgun blast was the only sound Doc needed to hear. He forced Molly out the back way, scattered the horses save for hers and his own, and left his other man beneath the stairway to wait for whoever returned. He and Molly rode, hard, back toward his waiting men.

Morgan saw the still open office door. He knew it wouldn't be long before some of her men would be checking the alley. He didn't see his horse . . . or anyone's. He turned to see if there was anybody behind him and the voice brought him forward again.

"Where's Jess?" It was Doc's other gunny.

"They got him . . . but he saved my life. Where's Doc?"

Even as Morgan spoke the words he knew they weren't doing him any good. The man's eyes had shifted to the Colt.

"You ain't no fuckin' dude at all . . . never were." The man stepped out of the shadows, smiled and pulled the trigger. The gun flew upwards, the shot buried itself in the thick wood of one of the stairs and the man dropped into a crumpled heap. Now the Colt was in Morgan's hand, but the man who stepped over the body of Doc's gunny was Trigg.

"This is getting to be a habit." Trigg walked up and handed Morgan a note.

My Apache woman reached Naschitti. He waits at the mission. My woman also reached Yates. He rides in the wrong direction.

Morgan looked up and smiled. "Don't take me wrong, Trigg, but you're sure as hell a man of few words and a helluva lot of action." Trigg smiled and scribbled something else.

Do I ride with you?

"No. Your note might just be what I need to convince Doc Henry that nothing has changed. Meantime, you've been to his stronghold. Keep clear of his men, wait 'til they've passed, and then ride back into Winchester Valley and wait." Trigg looked quizzical. "Yeah, I know it doesn't make sense but do it, Trigg . . . for Molly. I got a hunch

Doc Henry has an ace or two of his own. If he happens to get out of this alive, he'll head straight back there. You and your Sharps will be ready." Now Trigg smiled broadly and nodded. The two men shook hands and Morgan went in search of his horse. It was obvious that Trigg's presence had kept the rest of Molly's men off his back, and for that too he was grateful.

As he'd suspected, Doc Henry's anger was at it peak. Morgan ran into the gang less than five miles outside of Creede. It was probably only Molly's presence that kept Morgan from being gunned on the spot.

"Mahrgan . . . what . . ."

"Shut up, Molly!" Doc screamed. He had his own gun on Morgan and Charlie Bojack's was on him as well. Morgan had once again shed his Colt, slipping the gun into one saddle bag and the rig into the other.

"I'll let this do my thinking," Morgan said. He handed Doc the note Trigg had written. Doc had met Trigg only once, the day they first rode into Doc's stronghold. Nonetheless, he knew Trigg was Molly's man. He gave the note to her.

"That from your dummy?" She nodded. "What the hell happened down there, Butler?"

"Captain Torrance died a few days back. Some hot-headed West Pointer took over and decided to make a name for himself by killing Naschitti. The few men still there intended to detain me. Your man Jess cut down two of 'em and gave me my chance. Trigg helped out."

"And Jess?"

"Sorry, Jared. He didn't make it. Neither did your

other man, but it doesn't change anything. You saw that note and you saw what I got from Senor Valesquez. We need those guns. Now I'd suggest we break your men up into smaller groups and take a wide berth around Creede. We can't be sure what else may have happened, but there are no troops to worry about if we don't waste any time."

"I don't like it one Goddam bit, Doc," Charlie said. Morgan eyed some of the men. They too were restless and craning their necks in both directions looking for anything suspicious. Doc himself was staring straight into Morgan's face. Molly's stomach had a sinking feeling and her throat was bone dry.

"He give the orders now, Doc?" Morgan finally said.

"You're lyin' to me, dude. I know it. I can feel it. It's like poker when you know you got a hold hand."

The two men's eyes were locked in a silent struggle. Neither man blinked. Morgan knew Doc was right . . . it was a poker game and Doc held all the cards. All Morgan held was the bluff.

"Play it out, Doc. Play your hold hand. I'm calling you."

Doc frowned. "How you doin' that dude?"

"Your hundred thousand against my life."

Doc could feel the eyes upon him. Charlie's . . . the other men's near enough to have heard the exchange and . . . Molly's. The hair on the back of his neck bristled, and his cheeks felt flushed. Still, Morgan hadn't blinked. A wrinkle, just the smallest of wrinkles, appeared at one corner of Doc's mouth. His lips parted ever so slightly and the wrinkle spread across them into a half grin. He too was an old poker player.

"You take this pot, Butler . . . but the game ain't over. There'll be another hand dealt."

"We'd best ride," Morgan said. He turned his horse and as he did so, his eyes met Molly's for a split second. They both knew that the next hand Doc was talking about would be settled with Colts.

Miles away to the south, the half breed Brazo held up his arm and halted the column of men. They were at the entrance to Gato mission canyon. He turned to a gunny called Ferret and said, "You wait. I will ask to speak to Naschitti."

"This smells rotten," Ferret said. "This is a fuckin' box canyon and we ain't even sure them guns are in there."

Brazo smiled and pointed to the ground. There were deep ruts leading into the narrow gorge. "Wagons . . . heavy loaded." He nodded a self-confirmation. "The guns are there . . . but maybe army too. I will see."

Ferrett dismounted the men, all of them eyeing the canyon walls and the ridges above for any sign of trouble. Brazo rode carefully. He followed the tracks, but also looked for signs of shod horses . . . cavalry mounts. He saw none. Suddenly, almost as if by magic, two Apache warriors appeared in front of him. He could hear two more drop to the ground behind him. He smiled and raised one arm in a gesture of greeting. It was not returned, but one of the warriors motioned for him to follow.

Half a mile into the ever narrowing canyon, the party rounded a sharp bend. Brazo saw a line of army wagons—a dozen, perhaps fifteen. Near them stood a group of Indians. One of them he recognized at once as Naschitti.

Brazo dismounted, walked over and again offered a silent gesture of greeting. Naschitti's rifle butt was the reply and Brazo doubled over in pain and dropped to his knees.

"The dog of no color rides for Jared? Where is he?"

"Johnny's dead." Brazo struggled for breath enough to speak. He coughed. "Bush-whacked. Doc is tryin' to find his killers," Brazo lied.

"Naschitti thinks you have learned the white man's ways very well. You lie!" He kicked Brazo and then held the barrel of his rifle to the half breed's forehead. "The blue coats trapped my son. I believe it was because of Jared. Yesterday the blue coats rode into our land to kill us. I believe it was because of Jared. Today . . . you and not Jared come to deal. Why, half breed?"

"I swear to you, Naschitti, I speak only true words. I would not lie to my brother." Naschitti kicked him again.

"You are not my brother. You are no man's brother. You do not fly with the birds or run with the deer." Brazo was scared. He swallowed hard. He licked his parched lips and then raised his arm ever so slowly and pointed to the wagons.

"The rifles . . . as Jared promised. They're the proof. The cannon too and the gun of many bullets."

"Perhaps the rifles are no good. Perhaps they will not fire. Perhaps they will blow up in the faces of my warriors."

"No Naschitti, no! Open them, see for yourself."

"Now it is Naschitti who will say . . . no! Bring Jared's men into the canyon. Then we will open the boxes. They will fire the guns. Then I will believe your words." Brazo nodded, weakly.

Ferret and the others wanted no part of entering the canyon but they were also aware that Naschitti commanded more than a hundred braves. Running might prolong their lives but it most certainly wouldn't save them. Nearly an hour had passed before all of Jared's men were at the clearing near the mission. Above and all around them were Naschitti's warriors.

"You, half breed," Naschitti said, "you open the first box. You fire the first rifle."

Brazo nodded and waved. He moved over to the nearest wagon and, with the help of two of the men, opened the first case. They looked at each other with relief when they saw rifles. Brazo broke open an ammunition box. loaded the weapon, took aim at a cluster of rocks well up the side of one of the canyon walls and let go four rounds. The rocks disintegrated into dust. Brazo held up the rifle.

"Your proof, Naschitti." Now many of the other men rushed to the wagons and began breaking open cases. They simply wanted to complete the negotiations, get their payoff and ride out. It was not to be.

Many of the crates on the second layer had already been opened. What the men found were pieces of lead pipe. Brazo checked box after box. Two . . . four . . . seven. He began backing up. Slowly he turned and looked toward Naschitti. The Apache bent over, picked up something and then mounted his horse. He held up a length of lead pipe.

"Fire it . . . dog of no color."

"Naschitti . . . we didn't know . . . there's been
. . ." Naschitti's arm came down and the canyon was
suddenly filled with the roar and smoke of gun fire
and the less audible *twang* of bow strings and
whoosh of arrow and lance.

Jared's men huddled together and returned the
fire but in less than ten minutes, Gato canyon fell
silent again. Brazo, Ferret, three or four others tried
to slip out. Their ultimate fates made them regret
the effort. They would have died much quicker had
they stayed. By noon, the gun deal with Naschitti in
Gato canyon was over.

Doc Henry Jared's thoughts were running to
many things and the Gato deal was one of them. He
no longer trusted the man called Butler. He was not
certain of Molly, and he particularly didn't like the
idea of splitting his already inferior force. Doc had
spent time in the army and he knew the rule. Only
the element of time prevented him from riding into
Creede and snooping around. Instead, he kept Molly
with him and his small band, about seven men. He
sent Butler with a little larger group, a dozen, under
command of Charlie Bojack. Two other groups were
also formed for a total of twenty-eight guns.

One of the first groups which neared the trail
along the Rio Grande was the one led by Charlie
Bojack. Morgan's eyes scanned ahead carefully. He
was hoping the troopers were in place and hoping
even more that they wouldn't mistake this group for
the whole gang. He coudln't see any signs to
indicate they were even there, but Charlie wasn't
riding to the river until Doc ordered it.

"We wait here," he said to Morgan. Morgan nodded and continued his surveillance of the terrain, adding to it a possible escape route if things went suddenly sour.

The men in the second group were less cautious than Charlie. They appeared out of the woods, off trail, riding hard and loud. The instant they had mingled with Charlie's men, the old sergeant decided he had them all. Troopers stood up on both sides of them as well as to the front and rear and began firing.

Morgan caught Charlie a good, solid backhand swing to the chest and knocked him from his horse. At the same moment, he dug his spurs into the roan's flanks, jerked the big gelding's head hard to the right, and plunged into the trees. He felt the burning slash of a bullet as it dug a ridge high up on his left arm. Another severed the left stirrup link and Morgan had to shift his weight. A third grazed the horse and he snorted and seemed to dig harder for more speed.

Once out of the main line of fire, Morgan turned north and rode hard and low in the saddle. He worked the Bisley out of his saddlebag . . . and none too soon. Two men crashed through the brush just ahead of him. Doc's men. He cut them both down.

Less than a mile away, Doc Henry heard the shooting. He reined up. Suddenly a rider appeared before him. The rider spoke and Doc Henry's face wrinkled into a mask of hatred. He struck Molly a solid blow to the face and she slipped from her horse unconscious.

"Tie her to the saddle. We ride for the valley."

"The men?"

"To hell with the men!" Doc screamed.

Billy Frye was with the last group. It had stationed itself about midway between Doc's position and the rendezvous point when the shooting started.

"Ambush!" he screamed. He turned his horse and rode back toward Creede. As he did so, he yelled. "Every man for himself." The others took him at his word and scattered. Billy was counting on it. Doc had left two men behind to keep an eye on the girls, including Beth. He had to get to them before Doc did. Given Morgan's position, Billy was certain that he was already dead. Now, it was all up to Billy.

By the time Billy Frye had ridden around Creede, moving far more slowly than he wanted to, for fear of discovery, the gun fire behind him had stopped. Most of the men, he reckoned, had given up. Carefully, he gauged, the distance back to where Doc had left the women and tried to approach it from the back side. He found the spot but not the women. Even as he searched, he heard several lone riders gallop past on the nearby road. Stragglers, headed back to Winchester Valley. He sat down and wept.

11

Billy felt a hand clamped over his mouth and the cold steel of a gun barrel at his temple. He opened his eyes to find it was dark. He'd slipped into a sleep of utter fatigue. He blinked.

"It's me, Billy . . . Lee Morgan." Morgan released his grip. "No need for noise . . . just in case." Billy nodded. The day's events rushed back to his head. He sat up.

"They're gone . . . the girls. I . . ." Morgan was shaking his head. "I know. Doc got here first. By now they'll be back in the valley."

"They'll be *dead*. God! Oh God, Beth."

"Easy boy. Doc won't have killed them . . . not yet."

"Why the hell should we wait?"

"They're the bait, Billy . . . the only reason for me to ride back and face him."

"How can you be so sure?"

"Because I know how Doc thinks. Besides," Morgan added, standing up, "Doc will want me to watch them die . . . one by one. Particularly Molly."

Billy got to his feet.

"I'm riding with you."

"I'd counted on that," Morgan said. He smiled at Billy's look of shock.

"Why can't we get some help from the army?"

"We can . . . when Yates gets back. Right now there aren't enough troopers left. They've got their hands full keeping tabs on Doc's men."

"And when will Yates be back?"

"That's the problem, Billy, we don't know and we can't wait. I stayed out of sight and rode into Creede after dark. I spoke to the sergeant. He'll give Yates the word as soon as they ride in."

"You an' me . . . that's it?"

"And, if he didn't get spotted, Molly's man, Trigg."

"Doc had seven men with 'im. Top guns. I heard more later, five or six, mebbe."

Morgan motioned to Billy to follow him and they walked over to Morgan's horse. He lifted two sets of saddle bags from around its neck and handed them to Billy. They were heavy. Billy opened the flap on one of them.

"Dynamite!"

"Those bags and mine. Maybe we can cut down the odds a little."

They climbed the pass and found a decent spot to camp. It would have been both foolish and dangerous to try going down in the darkness. The two men hadn't spoken a word since they left their meeting place. They dined on cold beans and jerky, not daring to risk a fire. Shortly after midnight, a light but steady drizzle started to fall.

"Mister Morgan . . . you awake?"

"Yeah."

"You really think we got a chance o' savin' the girls?"

"If we work things right . . . mebbe we do, Billy."

"You got a plan?"

"Yeah . . . in a way," Morgan lied.

"I got somethin' itchin' at me," Billy said. He didn't wait for Morgan to respond. "I come near to high-tailin' today . . . even though I knowed my sister was likely in there . . . or already daid."

"What stopped you?"

"Ain't real sure. Even if we save the women an' git Doc, I'm facin' jail. I rode with 'im. Done what he done."

"Kill anybody, boy?"

"Nope. Doc wouldn't let me ride gun for him. Don't think I'm good enough yet."

"You're good enough, Billy . . . you've just got to put aside your judgments. If a man wants to kill you, then you've got to want to live."

"You mean I gotta want to kill *him*?"

"No. I mean just what I said. You've got to value life more than death. It just so happens, in that case, the life you value most is your own. In this case, right now, maybe the life you value most is Beth's. You can't win a gun fight just because you're better. Remember that there's never a horse that couldn't be rode and never a rider that couldn't be throwed."

"Meanin' there's always somebody better'n you?"

"Yeah. Somewhere. But that's okay providing the only thing he cares about is proving it. Then, Billy, you got the edge."

"You ever faced a man better'n you?"

"Faster mebbe . . . but with the wrong reasons for trying me."

"Ya know, Mister Morgan. I think I understand what you're sayin'. Doc, he tol' me oncest that Charlie Bojack was the fastest man he'd ever knowed with a gun. I asked him . . . was Charlie faster'n him? He tol' me that Charlie was . . . but in a showdown Doc said he'd win 'cause Charlie wouldn't want to kill him. Doc said he wouldn't give a damn 'bout killin' Charlie."

"That's about it, Billy, that's an edge. Just remember, it's not only the edge. Doc Henry don't give a damn about life at all."

"Even his own?"

"It's never really been put on the line. He hasn't had to make the decision."

"But what if he did have to?" Billy asked. He was sitting up now and looking at Morgan. "What if it was you an' your edge an' him? What if he decided his life was more important than yours an' what if he was faster'n you?"

"I'd kill him, Billy."

"Damn, Mister Morgan . . . how the hell can you be so sure?"

"Because he'd have to take the time to make his decision. Mine's already made. I'd kill him in the difference."

The rain had stopped. A silky mist crawled along the valley floor. As they rode toward it, Billy commented that he thought it looked like snow. By the time they reached it, it was gone. The sun was half way to noon and Lee Morgan's thoughts were miles and years from Winchester Valley.

He remembered back . . . back to the Spade Bit. Then too, he was riding in to face one of the best . . . a man with the speed, the skill, the edge. He was looking for Buckskin Frank Leslie. He was looking for his father. No, not his father but the man who'd sired him and then left. Then Lee thought there was a difference. He also thought Frank Leslie was living on his reputation. Lee couldn't gun the old man. He'd had the chance. He couldn't.

The next time he saw Frank Leslie he also saw the edge. Harvey Logan had come looking for Lee. A greenhorn kid with a nasty black snake whip and a vast draw.. Harvey Logan was faster. Harvey found Lee, but he found Buckskin Frank Leslie first. It was over in the blink of an eye. Frank still had the edge, but he'd slowed just a hair. He died that day. He left his son a borrowed name . . . Lee. He left him the name of his unwed mother . . . Morgan. He warned him about the black snake whip. He left the boy a ranch . . . the Spade Bit. He left him half a reputation, but most of all, Frank Leslie willed to Lee Morgan . . . the edge.

"Smoke, Mister Morgan."

"Wha . . ." Morgan must have almost been dozing in the saddle. His eyes opened, his muscles rippled to respond to the signals his brain sent them. *Danger!* Then reason . . . he shook free of the cobwebs of his memory.

"Up ahead . . . comin' from the valley." Morgan saw it. He held up his hand and Billy Frye reined up. Morgan looked over the lay of the land. He pointed wordlessly to a stand of Aspen near the river.

"You stay here, Billy. Today and tonight. Keep the horses out of sight. No fire. No nerves. If I'm not back by sun-up," Morgan now turned and looked Billy in the eye, "then you do what you have to do."

"You ain't goin' into the valley alone . . . not on foot?"

"I've got to look . . . get some idea what we're up against. You sit. I'll be back."

Billy watched Morgan change his clothes. He wasn't a dude anymore. He carefully slipped cartridges into his rig's belt, checked the Bisley, and half smiled as he caught a glimpse of the initials W.F.L., William Frank Leslie. Morgan slipped the Colt into the holster, pulled it, put it back, pulled it again. Billy thought it was like breathing . . . natural, easy, smooth.

Morgan checked over the Winchester with equal care. He slipped a cartridge belt of rifle ammunition over his shoulder, then untied his bedroll, laid it down, and rolled it open. Inside, Billy saw a Black Snake bull whip. Hand woven. Snake skin, leather grip with silver inlay. Eight thongs, silver tipped, at the business end.

Morgan eyed Billy. His own father's words echoed again in his ears. "*Better shoot a man than use that thing on him.*" Morgan laid it behind him in a single, easy move of his arm. He eyed a tree. Six feet up there was a bare branch with a knot of wood on its end. Billy's eyes shifted to the limb. Morgan flexed his grip, made a slight dipping motion with his wrist and then a long, smooth forward motion. There was an almost inaudible *swish* in the air. A sharp, short-lived *craack* . . . the limb was still there. . . the little knot of wood was gone.

He could still use the whip. Some men deserved worse than shot. Some deserved to hang, but not all of them could. The whip might make it possible for *one* man to hang . . . or so thought Lee Morgan about Doc Henry Jared.

Doc Henry sat at his desk. He was swilling whisky. The window shades were pulled. Doc fingered his hand gun as his mind conjured up fuzzy pictures of Lee Morgan standing before him. Johnny Jared had been fast; Doc had taught him. Doc wanted Morgan . . . the old way. Just the two of them. He took another swallow of whisky, sloshed it back and forth between his cheeks, and then swallowed. It wouldn't be that way, he knew that. He'd take Morgan alive . . . partly alive anyway. Then there were the women. Morgan could watch before he died.

The door opened, easy . . . quiet. Doc looked up. It was Charlie Bojack.

"All the whores is locked up an' watched. Took their clothes off'n 'em." He laughed, nervously. "*Keerist!* The boys was cuttin' cards jist fer the privilege o' keepin' an eye on 'em."

"Molly?"

"Nope. Did jist what you ask, Doc. She's up in yore room, hawg tied."

"Anybody else ride in?" Doc asked.

" 'Fraid not. Two o' the boys rode out yesterday . . . found four o' the men 'bout two, mebbe three miles apart. All shot with a buffalo gun."

"The sumbitch with the Sharps. Who the hell is he?"

"Cully Bright thinks he put a slug into 'im . . .

ain't fer sure, though, but Cully got on it. So did Hightower. Want we should go lookin'?"

"Hell no! If the sumbitch is hit or dead, it's over. If he ain't, he'd get ya one at a time. We'll wait it out."

"Doc . . . well . . . some o' the boys figure we're waitin' fer nothin' but trouble. Army's bound to come after us soon. Well . . . they ain't too sure Lee Morgan'll come in, not even fer that Irish bitch."

"I don't give a Goddam what they think, Charlie, nor you neither. You all want to ride out, fuck you. Ride out. Morgan'll be here . . . and when he gets here, I'll be waitin'." Doc picked up his pistol and then got to his feet. "How 'bout you, Charlie?"

"I'll be here, Doc. You know that."

"I don't know nothin' fer sure anymore . . . 'cept I'm gonna have the personal pleasure o' killin' Lee Fuckin' Morgan."

"Okay, Doc. If that's your word, then that's what'll happen. We got eleven men. They's only two o' them." Doc said nothing else and Charlie Bojack slipped quietly out.

Doc took another long pull of the bottle. He wiped his mouth with his shirt sleeve and picked up his pistol. "C'mon," he whispered to himself, "c'mon to Doc, you sumbitch."

Morgan spent most of the afternoon climbing. The sun was already behind Pole Creek mountain when he finally settled onto an overhang that had a small cave behind it. The shadows were long and purple, but below Morgan could see all of Winchester Valley.

He could see the curl of smoke from Doc Henry's

house. The smoke from the other building, the one housing the men, was thicker, darker, and spread out, creating a haze. Two men stood watch at a third building. Morgan smiled slightly. The women. They were still alive.

Morgan counted stock. Fifteen riding horses, four pack mules. A dozen men? He wondered. It seemed a fair amount, but Doc could have twenty in hiding. Then again . . . maybe there were only six. He stowed his gear, got himself situated for any emergency, and half settled in for the long night ahead.

A rock, it was small, almost a pebble, dropped beside him. The Colt came up. He could see a dark patch dart between the boulders above him.

"Damn," he whispered to himself. "Who the hell dogged me?" He wondered if it might be Trigg. He hoped so. Another pebble. Footsteps, some gravel slid. He levelled the Colt. Whoever it was didn't seem to care about being heard.

"Mor-gun . . . Mor-gun?" Morgan got to his feet. He stepped nearer the edge of the drop for a better look up the narrow path that led back to the ridge above him. He saw his visitor.

"Jeezus. Who the hell are you?"

"Tonsika . . . I am the woman of the man who does not speak." Trigg's Apache! She'd dogged him and Billy . . . then him. Why? "I find the Buffalo gun man here?"

"No." Morgan helped her the last few feet. He got her inside the small cave. "You shouldn't be here. You could get us both killed."

"No one follows Tonsika. I come to find . . ."

"Yeah, yeah, Trigg. His name is *Trigg.*"

"Tuh-rig?"

"Close enough. Did you follow him or me?"

"I follow you. I come from the blue coats with a message."

"*Yates?*"

"The boy blue coat," she pointed to her shoulders, "with gold thread here."

"Yates. What about him? What's the message?"

"In two suns he is to meet with his blue coat chief . . . he say Gen-rul Coombs."

"Then what, Tonsika? Then what?"

"Many pony soldiers ride here to the Uncompahgre. They will kill the evil white eyes."

"How many days . . . uh . . . how many suns before they do that?"

"The boy blue coat tells Tonsika . . . four . . . maybe five."

"Shit!"

"Tuh-rig?"

"I don't know. Dead maybe. Down there," Morgan pointed, "maybe."

"This night . . . I stay with Mor-gun."

"Yeah, that's how it looks."

Morgan slept hard for a couple of hours. Then it rained. The wind blew in and he and Tonsika both got wet. The rain stopped. He could hear, ever so faintly, men's laughter from Doc's compound far below. Tonsika was cold. She stripped. He turned his bedroll to the dry side.

Tonsika was young . . . *very* young. Morgan tried to put his desire out of his body and her age out of his mind. She was too close . . . it was too cold and, Morgan thought, they'd both likely be dead in a few days. If there was still a doubt, Tonsika removed it. She moved his hand to her tiny breast. It was firm, almost hard. It had not yet fully developed. Morgan looked into her eyes. They revealed only an adolescent yielding. Tonsika was exploring . . . searching for her womanhood. She was trapped between little girl and passionate lover. Morgan was her choice only because he was there.

He moved his hand and lowered his head until he could rest it on her body. His tongue flicked the tiny nipple, already hardened from the cold air. She moaned softly as he continued his ministrations. His fingers too began an exploratory movement along her inner thighs. She reacted by spreading them. He continued licking and sucking at her nipple and with his free hand, reached beneath and around her to toy with the other one.

His other hand found her pubic hair. It was fine, soft and covered very little. He was more accustomed to the thick, wiry hair of a mature woman. He found it fascinating and stroked it for several minutes before his fingers dropped lower.

"Go inside me . . . Mor-gan." She whispered the words. Morgan replied, "Shh! In time Tonsika . . . in time." He found the tender flesh between her legs and parted it gently. He was surprised at the moistness. He rubbed. Tonsika's back stiffened and arched, pressing her pussy against his fingers.

He found the bud of her passion. The clitoris was the smallest Morgan had ever touched. Merely a pimple . . . but far more sensitive than that of a white woman. The combination of his breast play and his light touch between her legs prompted a premature climax. Morgan cursed himself for not realizing what might happen.

Tonsika let out a little howl. Her legs went farther apart and she bent them at the knees as she pushed against his hand. She gasped. He could feel more liquid, thicker and slimy . . . like cactus juice. Her body went limp. She opened her eyes. She smiled.

"Again . . . Mor-gun." She raised her legs into the air, spread them as far apart as possible and simply waited. Morgan didn't. He resumed his touch, his stroking and the use of his tongue. Slowly, he shifted his own position until he was on his knees between her legs. He lowered his head and his tongue found her navel. He circled it and then traced a path below it until he felt the line of her hair. He moved from side to side now, flicking his tongue over the protrusions that were her hip bones. He lowered his head, licking at the inside of her thighs. Then he thrust home.

His tongue moved sideways first, then up and down. She closed her legs around his head and pushed. He licked her clitoris. The body stiffened again, held its suspended position for a few seconds and then relaxed again. This time there was no moan, nothing but a body reflex. Morgan raised up. Tonsika smiled again.

"Go inside me, Mor-gun . . . *please.*"

Morgan removed his pants and dropped his underdrawers to his ankles. Tonsika spread her legs for the third time and Morgan was ready. He was concerned about hurting her . . . she was so small and Morgan didn't lack from either thickness or length. He needn't have worried. He thought it was like slipping his cock into a half-ripened honeydew melon. Moist, very tight and without a bottom. He began a rhythm, and soon Tonsika had found it and joined him. They were fucking . . . pure, simple fucking. He couldn't remember the last time he'd done that. He'd forgotten the *feel* of it . . . the pure enjoyment of sex between man and woman which used only the tools God had given them for the act.

Morgan and Tonsika remained connected for a long time. Slow, loving, tender strokes. She grew more passionate with each and Morgan's juices built to a crescendo exactly timed with that of the Indian maiden. They burst forth together, writhing bodies no longer two . . . but melding into one. Oblivious to the cold . . . to artificial stimuli . . . a man . . . a woman . . . a climax of physical passion.

Afterwards, they kept each other warm, huddling close but saying nothing. Morgan finally raised up to his elbows, leaned over and very gently kissed Tonsika on the mouth. He pulled away, looked into her eyes and said, "Thank you. You made pleasant memories for me tonight." Tonsika just smiled.

12

Tonsika was gone! Morgan was furious at himself. He'd never even heard her leave. He'd told Billy Frye he'd be back by sun-up. He guessed it was eight thirty, maybe later. He didn't excuse himself for being bone weary from the climb and drained from fucking half the night. Even if they were legitimate reasons, they could cost him . . . or other people . . . their lives. He resolved not to let such a thing happen again.

His stomach was growling. He wanted coffee, but settled for half a can of beans. He readied his gear and then studied Doc's compound again. He could see some action but nothing out of the ordinary and, more important, nothing to indicate the arrival of more men.

The trip back down the mountain seemed much easier, barely more than a morning stroll. He stopped to rest and estimated he was now within three miles of where he'd left Billy. He hoped the boy would have sense enough to do nothing immediately. By now, Morgan was sure that Billy would be plenty worried . . . perhaps even panicky, but with luck, he'd still be at the camp. Morgan had also considered the possibility of Tonsika finding Billy.

He had barely resumed his trip when an ear-shattering blast reverberated through the canyon. He thought it had come from behind him, but such sound echoed so in the mountains, it was difficult to tell.

"Stupid little sonuvabitch," Morgan mumbled. He'd concluded that Billy had put some of the dynamite to use. He'd barely recuperated from the explosion when another tore loose, followed by two more. Morgan made a quick decision. He hid most of what he was carrying beneath a boulder, took only his Winchester, and broke into a trot. He figured he'd either cross trail with Billy or get back to their camp ahead of him.

He'd gone nearly two miles when another sound, more faint but just as easily recognized, caught up to him. It was the deep, guttural discharge of a Sharps . . . .50 calibre!

"Trigg?" Morgan turned. Another shot . . . a rifle. A Henry maybe or Winchester. There was the Sharps again. Morgan made his decision. Billy was a maybe, but Trigg was alive. He turned to run in the direction of the gunshots.

"Mister Morgan . . . Mister Morgan." He wheeled. There was Billy, mounted, and with the roan gelding in tow.

"I'm a little late," Morgan said, "sorry."

"I thought all of the noise was prob'ly you."

"Well it wasn't," Morgan said, as he jumped into the saddle, "so let's find out who the hell did make it."

Moving fast, but carefully, deep in the woods, Morgan and Billy finally reached a point where the trail into the valley narrowed. They saw no one, but they did find the cause for the blasting . . . and the results.

"Goddam!" It was all Morgan could manage. Billy couldn't even muster up that much. The trail was completely blocked with huge boulders. A lone man would have a tough go at getting over them, let alone doing so without being seen on the other side.

"Army boys can't get in now, can they, Mister Morgan?"

"Oh yeah, Billy," Morgan replied, sarcastically, "if they want to take the same losses the Mexicans took at the Alamo. Shit!"

"An' we don't know how many's in there, either."

"Yes we do." Both men wheeled around at the sound of the strange voice. Morgan's Colt was in his hand, but his mouth dropped open. There stood Tonsika and next to her . . . Trigg. "I overheard one o' them this marnin' . . . he figured the eleven of 'em . . . plus Doc Henry himself . . . could hold off the army long enough if it came to that. There's two less than that now."

Morgan walked up to Trigg. "You talk, you sonuvabitch . . . and you talk *Irish*."

Trigg grinned. "There's a reason for that, Mahrgan . . . I am Irish. I'm Molly's big brother, come over with our sister."

"Holy Jeezus!"

Trigg motioned with his head for the two men to follow him. "We'd best get out of sight. They could be watchin' too. I've moved me spot again an' I think it's good enough for the lot of us. I'll fill in all the holes when we get there."

Trigg . . . or whatever his name was . . . had picked out one hell of a spot to hide. He could no longer simply pick off Doc's men from there, but if they happened to ride out and find him, they'd play hell ever getting to him. It was a cave, high up, good shelter, and an excellent view below. There was open ground for nearly half a mile leading to its base. And it was only a mile to the main trail.

"Helluva fortress, Trigg," Morgan said.

"Name's not Trigg. It's Patrick Sean Terrence O'Flynn." He grinned. "Covered me father, grandfather, and me uncle." Morgan was listening, but he was also looking. He was more than a little surprised. There was fresh meat, tinned food, whisky, some medicine, several rifles and hand guns, appropriate ammuntion, coal oil, lamps, and half a dozen cases of dynamite.

"You've proven to be a damned handy man to have around," Morgan finally said. Then he pointed to the various items and added, "But I don't think you're this damned good."

"Hardly, Mahrgan. I've been slippin' in an' out o' here for more'n six months. I knew there'd be a time . . . a day o' reckonin'. I'm thankin' the Good Lawrd I'll still be around to see it."

"The dummy act, Trigg . . . uh, O'Flynn. What about that? Just covering the Irish accent?"

"Call me Paddy . . . most do." Then he nodded. "The dummy act, as you call it, was a God-send. It did cover up the accent, sure . . . but I didn't plan it." He pulled down the neckerchief around his throat and revealed an ugly, deep scar. "Minie ball. Took quite a chunk o' me throat. I couldn't talk for quite a spell. It happened on the same raid that took me other sister. I managed to crawl off and hide."

"You and Molly figured out the rest?" Paddy nodded. "Sorry I haven't introduced you . . . this is Billy Frye."

"I know about Billy Frye and his sister. We'll get her out, boy . . . Molly an' the others too."

Tonsika cooked some breakfast. The cave was deep and her Apache upbringing paid its own dividends. She could build a fire and cook on it with almost no smoke at all. The quartet of friends ate and then Billy fell into a deep sleep. Tonsika climbed a nearby rock ledge and stood watch while Morgan and Paddy O'Flynn split a pint of whisky.

"I can't help wanting to call you Trigg," Morgan said. "Maybe we should keep it that way."

"No matter to me. It's a name I'll not likely ever forget, anyway."

"There's another little matter," Morgan said. "I'm not sure just how you'll take it, but we'd best get it out."

Trigg smiled. "If you're meanin' the Indian girl, she already told me. I've no mark on her, Mahrgan, nor she on me."

"I'm glad you're on my side," Morgan said. "I got a hunch you'd be as mean an enemy as you are a good friend . . . and a good man."

"It's as much trainin' as anythin', Mahrgan. I was an officer in the Queen's Own fer fifteen years."

"Jeezus! That explains a lot of things," he gestured at the surroundings with a sweep of his arm, "this among them."

"It might help, but maybe not. Not if Doc Henry kills an' runs. There is a back way out o' that valley."

"He won't take it, Trigg. He knows I'm coming. He wants me."

"It's the only thing we've got goin' for us, Mahrgan. The only chance we've got to save Molly and the others."

"It's enough."

"Have you got a plan, Mahrgan?"

Morgan grinned now. "Sure, but I'd damn sight rather use yours."

"It's had to be changed some, you know."

"I'd say that's one hell of an understatement. The Goddam army fucked everything up back down on the Rio Grande. I figured to be chasing Doc Henry and maybe one or two of his gunnies . . . but not a dozen and not with him holding the women or holed up in this valley."

"Don't blame the army fer everything, Mahrgan. He had some help."

"From where? Who?"

"I can't answer that one yet . . . but he did. I got that much out of one of his men, a young one I shot up two days back. He told me about everything he knew. Too bad my shootin' was better'n my doctorin'. He didn't make it."

"What's your plan, Trigg?"

"Well, now that you an' the boy are here, I'd say it was best to send a message on back to the army. The Indian girl can do that. Get them movin' a bit faster, maybe."

"I'll buy that, but then what? I figured to slip into the compound and do as much damage as possible. Maybe entice Doc Henry into an open confrontation."

"The dynamite?"

"Yeah. I've got some myself."

"Nothin' wrong with the plan on paper, Mahrgan. But it has to include gettin' one or more o' his men *ever'time*. Right now it's three to one an' I don't think they'll be comin' out again so's I can pick 'em off with the old Buffalo gun."

"Agreed." Billy Frye sat bolt upright. Both men thought he'd been sleeping hard. "Someone's comin'," he said. Both his guns were drawn and even Morgan was impressed with the speed. A moment later, Tonsika entered the cave.

"A white man . . . alone near the rocks on the trail. He carries the white man's sign of talk."

"A white flag?" She nodded. "Then they know they can be seen."

"Yes, Mahrgan," Trigg said, shaking his head in bewilderment, "an' they still expect we'll act as honorable men . . . even when they don't."

"Are you suggesting that we don't?"

"Not at all. We've no choice while they hold the women. Well then, let's have a look."

The closing of the narrow trail into Winchester Valley with the blasting of the rocks was a two-edged sword. It would make it impossible for any sizeable number of men to get into the valley without being seen, but it also limited the number coming out to one or two. By the time Trigg and Morgan reached a spot where they could see the trail, the man had gone. There was a pole in the ground which bore the white flag and a note. Tonsika walked down and retrieved it.

Sun up tomorrow, Morgan. You and me, right

here. Every hour goes by you don't show, I kill
a girl.

"Shit! I've been afraid of this," Morgan said.
"He's got a hold hand again."

"An' more back-up guns than we've got," Trigg
added. "He won't face you without them, Mahrgan
. . . you know that, don't you?"

"Yeah, Trigg, I know it."

"Me'n Trigg here will back you. We can keep
under cover."

"We could that, boy . . . but we can't be sure we'd
get 'em all."

"And if I don't show?" Morgan wadded up the
note and threw it down. "He'll do it, Trigg. He'll do
it just to prove he can."

"Then we'd best plan on goin' in there tonight and
gettin' those girls out."

"Sure, Trigg . . . just like that."

"Young Billy, here. I was thinkin'. They don't
know what's happened to the lad. So he's a day or
two late gettin' back. If he rides in, they'll not argue
with 'im . . . will they?" Morgan's eyes lit up. So did
Billy's. "We can sweeten the pot a bit, too. I'll give
the boy my Buffalo gun. He can tell his own story."

"I can do it, Mister Morgan. I *can.* He's right an' I
can keep 'em all busy long enough fer you to get the
women. I know I can."

"It just might work," Morgan said.

"An' we'll get the girl here on the way back to the
army . . . just in case."

Less than an hour later, Tonsika, using Billy's
horse, slipped through the woods and headed
toward Creede and safety. Morgan climbed to some

high rocks after bidding his farewell to Billy. There, he fired half a dozen shots from his Colt and his Winchester. Below him, Trigg fired the old Sharps once, twice . . . and then again. Billy scrambled up the pile of boulders at the entrance to the canyon. He let himself be seen, fired behind him several times, and then scrambled down the other side. He holstered his guns, put the old Sharps over his shoulder and started walking.

"Hold it, kid." Bill turned. He saw Frank Potts, one of Doc's top hands.

"It's me Frank, Billy Frye." By then, several other men had reached the spot. Charlie Bojack was out front.

"Goddam if it ain't the kid. We thought you was dead." Now Charlie spotted the Sharps. "Where'd you git that?" he asked. His voice had changed tone. Billy knew he was suspicious.

"From the son-fo-a-bitch that tried to way-lay me with it," Bill answered. His voice was firm, cool . . . even proud in tone.

"Is that right? We'll see, kid, we'll see. You tell that one to Doc."

Two men remained behind . . . the front line watch. Billy took note of their positions. He'd already formulated an addition to the plan which even Trigg and Morgan didn't know about. A few minutes later, Charlie ushered Billy into Doc's office.

"Well, sumbitch . . . if it ain't the gun-slingin' kid." Doc spotted the Sharps and frowned.

"Claims he got the sharp shootin' bastard," Charlie said.

Billy's head jerked sharply toward Charlie Bojack. "I don't claim nothin', Charlie. I did git 'im."

Doc grinned. "An' you brung in his piece to prove it."

"Hell no. I got it 'cause I wanted it. He's got no more use for it."

"An' nobody else was out there? Morgan wasn't out there? You just picked off the sharp shooter, walked up and took his piece and here you are."

Billy stood the Sharps against the wall and backed up. "You callin' me a liar?" Doc was clearly surprised.

"You got a heap o' grit all o' the sudden, boy."

"It come from ridin' with yellow bellies." Charlie Bojack took a step toward Billy. Doc held up his arm.

"What yellow bellies you talkin' about, boy?"

"Them what I was with when the army hit us. Them you hired an' trusted. Most scattered like chickens. Damn near come gettin' kilt because of 'em." Billy rattled off the names of two men he knew had died. "They was the only ones besides me what fought. I barely got away, and when I finally got back this far an' that bastard shot my horse . . . well, I just plain got mad." He turned toward Charlie. "An' I'm mad right now. Don't need nobody callin' me a liar."

"That sharp shooter took out some good men, damn good men. Only one got through was Cully. He did enough shootin' so's Hightower could make it too. Now Cully, he's a better man than you, boy."

"Who says? You, Doc?"

"You got a smart mouth, boy." Doc walked over and backhanded Billy. At the same instant, he felt the barrel of a Colt against his belly.

"I come back, Doc, 'cause you did me right. But I'm no boy anymore. I did what I said I did an' I ain't takin' no slappin' around." Billy backed up and looked Doc square on. "Not even from you."

Doc Henry grinned. "Sumbitch! You *have* growed boy, a whole fuckin' heap in a week. Why I bet you figure you could take on ol' Charlie here now."

Billy holstered his gun. "I got no fight with Charlie, an' I don't need to be provin' I'm better'n him. Only thing I'm willin' to prove is what I tol' you. I got the Sharps man. You want, I'll ride out an' fetch his carcass back here."

Billy Frye had just turned in the performance of his life. It rivalled anything ever done by Edwin Booth or the great Sarah Bernhardt. Within himself, Billy felt it. But even more surprising, he felt, at that moment, as though he could have taken out Charlie Bojack and Doc Henry Jared too, if it had come to that.

"Sumbitch!" Doc laughed. "Hell, boy . . . you showed some real guts just now. Yessir, real guts. You got nothin' to prove to me. I believe ever' word ya said." Billy smiled. Doc stopped smiling. "An' one more thing, *boy* . . . you ever pull on me ag'in, you're fuckin' *dead*. You unnerstan' me?" Doc's sudden attack on Billy's manhood had its affect.

"Yeah, Doc. Sure. I . . . I'm sorry." He glanced at Charlie Bojack. Charlie too was sneering. They still held him in contempt. He felt the fire of anger and hatred in his belly, but Morgan's words were in his ears: "Value life . . . value life." He'd have a chance at them again . . . another time . . . another place.

Billy now played his own ace in the hole. He'd picked up the wadded note from Doc, unseen by either Morgan or Trigg. He pulled it from his vest pocket and handed it to Doc. Doc read. He looked up. He was truly impressed.

"Where'd you git this boy?"

"The man with the Sharps had it tucked in his shirt pocket. I went through his clothes, lookin' fer who he might be. I ain't seen 'im before . . . nowhere."

"You didn't see nobody else out there, no tracks . . . *nothin'*?"

"No, Doc. I rode in clean. They wasn't nobody out there but the man that owned this." He picked up the Sharps and held it out.

"Sumbitch! Morgan *ain't* out there."

"You don't know that for sure, Doc."

"Yeah, I do, Charlie. I do now. This here boy ain't lyin' to me. I got no *feelin'* about it."

The *edge,* Billy was thinking. There goes Doc Henry's *edge.* "Doc, lemme go do some snoopin' out there." Billy walked to the window and peered up at the sky. "There's enough daylight left. I know where I left that old man. Lemme see if'n I can find where he was camped. Who he was, mebbe."

"Yeah, boy . . . good idea. You do that. You take my horse too." When Bill was gone, Charlie Bojack stood quiet for a minute and then he hit one fist against the open palm of his other hand.

"I don't like it, Doc. It stinks like the shit house."

"Ever'thing stinks to you, Charlie."

"I was right before . . . right about that dude. I knowed I'd see 'im somewhere. Lee Morgan! I shoulda remembered."

"Yeah, Charlie, you *shoulda.* That's what I pay ya fer." Doc sat down. He took a drink. "I'm gonna kill 'im, Charlie . . . one way or another. The sumbitch is good, real good. Beat Johnny.''

"You figger he's better'n you, Doc?''

"Fact is, Charlie . . . I ain't too fuckin' sure about it.'' Doc took another pull on the bottle. "But it makes no never mind. I don't figure to face 'im alone. I just want 'im dead. Him, an' that Irish whore an' her girls.''

"Then what, Doc?''

"Then we clear out. Mexico, mebbe. We'll find us some good men. We'll be back.''

Billy Frye made double certain he wasn't followed. He'd had no trouble getting out of the compound and expected even less getting back in. Now he was Doc's man . . . at least for the moment. He tethered his horse well away from the trail leading to the cave and made his way quickly over the path until he was close enough to toss a rock at the cave's entrance. He did so and Trigg peered around the entrance wall.

"It's Billy Frye.'' Trigg waved. Inside, Billy quickly described the events at the compound. He had observed two men guarding the entry to the valley and two watching the building where the women were being held. "Get them four,'' he finally said, "an' it'll be five to three.''

"Not quite that easy,'' Morgan said. "The instant that happens, we've got to get those women the hell out of there.''

"That's true enough, Mahrgan. But young Billy here is right. If Doc has swallowed his story that you're not around and I'm dead, then we've got to do somethin' fast. He'll soon figure out you're not comin' without the whole damned army behind you. He's just liable to kill those women . . . or decide to move out the back way."

"I was thinkin' about that ridin' in," Billy offered. "I got a plan." Both men looked at him, then at each other.

"Let's hear it, Billy."

"You write a note to Trigg. Tell 'im to sit tight and keep 'em pinned down 'til you can steer the army away an' then git here. Uh . . . today's Thursday. Write that if ever'thing goes accordin' to plan that you'll be ridin' in Saturday mornin' early."

"Then you'll take it back to Doc."

Billy nodded. "That's what I'm out here for, to snoop around. I think he'll believe what I bring back."

"Sounds to me like the boy's makin' sense."

"Not this time," Morgan said. "Doc Henry will want to see your body, your camp, *everything,* if Billy goes back with a note like that. It's no good. We're going to have to slip in, try to cut the odds, get the women and get out. We might even have to give up Doc in the bargain."

Rocks, jostled loose by someone, suddenly slipped from the ledge outside the cave and rattled down the hill. All three men levelled their guns at the entrance. In a moment, they were looking into the face of Tonsika. She half smiled, took a step forward, staggered and then fell. High on her back, between her shoulder blades, protruded the broken shaft of an Apache arrow.

Trigg moved quickly to treat her wound, assisted by Morgan. Several times they had to force her to lie still. Trigg finally managed removal of the arrow head itself. It had been deep. Morgan had seen such wounds many times. He looked into Trigg's face. Trigg's head moved from side to side, almost imperceptibly.

"No blue coats . . . Tonsika failed her Tuh-rug."

"Stay quiet, girl."

"Naschitti . . . he comes. All whites are his enemies." She coughed. Time was short. Tonsika reached Trigg's lips with her fingers as he started to speak again. Morgan knelt near her now too. "Naschitti will come with the sun . . . many braves . . . many guns."

"Tonsika . . . where will Naschitti come from?"

"From . . . from where the sun sleeps."

Tonsika fell into unconciousness. It was a sleep from which she would not awaken. The three men all knew it. She had never reached Creede. Naschitti's warriors were converging on Winchester Valley from all directions.

"Looks to me like Naschitti is goin' to do to Doc Henry what we'd like to do."

"If he gets the chance, Billy. His main force will come through the Uncompahgre from the west. He'll no doubt attack here first . . . draw the fire of whoever is in the valley . . . test the strength."

"The girls!"

"Yeah Billy. The girls."

"I . . . I didn't think."

"I knew it wouldn't take you long. Life, Billy . . . their lives or our hatred of Doc Henry."

"Well," Trigg said, drying his eyes as he shifted his gaze from Tonsika's form, "we've got no bloody choice, have we?"

"Not really. We either team up with Doc, and he

lets us . . . or we're all goners."

"Doc won't believe this," Billy said. "Not even from me. It's worse than the note . . . he won't believe it. He won't."

"Easy, Billy . . . don't lose your grip now. We need you. We need each other."

"But how? How do we convince Doc Henry?"

Trigg had been at the cave's entrance. He'd heard something. He called Morgan and Billy to his side and pointed. On the trail they saw three Apache warriors.

"He'll bloody well believe *that.*"

"How far ahead o' the main body you figger 'em for, Morgan?"

"The main force is with Naschitti off west. I'd say three or four miles back there's probably forty, mebbe fifty Apache."

"Let's get it over with," Trigg said.

"Billy, slip back to your horse. If one of 'em gets away from us, cut him at the trail. We'll give you two minutes."

The three Apache warriors were taken out with ease, and the firing drew the attention of Doc's men. Billy scampered back into the compound; it would still be better for Doc to believe Billy was riding with him. Doc's own men brought in Trigg, Morgan, and the Apache bodies.

Billy reported to Doc Henry that he had encountered the two men while searching the area for the camp of the sharpshooter. Billy said his only chance to run had been when the Apaches attacked. Charlie Bojack didn't believe him, but Doc went outside.

"I knowed you come, you bastard. You figger to

scare ol' Doc off with some Apache shootin'?"

"There's no way out, Doc. The main force, Naschitti . . . he'll ride in from the west with the sun tomorrow. First, you'll get hit at the gorge. The boulders will help but the only chance any of us has is being ready."

"Git down, Morgan. Let's you 'n' me settle it." He grinned. "One more gun either way ain't gonna matter . . . now is it?" Morgan dismounted.

"I suppose not, Doc. It's your hand again. Play it . . . I'll call you."

One of Doc's men from the entry gorge rode up fast. "Apaches, thirty, mebbe forty of 'em. Jeezus! They've built a fire, they're dancin' around hootin' and hollerin'. They'll be hittin' us fast, Doc."

Doc Henry looked at the man and frowned. He looked into Trigg's eyes and then at Morgan.

"I've got some dynamite," Morgan said. "The army's due here in two or three days. All we have to do is hold 'til then."

"Sure, Morgan. Then the army gits me instead o' the Apaches. That what you want?"

"If we hold . . . and if the army gets here . . . they'll have their hands full of Naschitti's warriors. Once they've distracted the Apache, you and I can settle our differences. We'll have plenty of time, Doc."

"You fucked Naschitti . . . not me."

Morgan laughed. "Then you hunt him out and tell him that, Doc. And make him believe it."

"I say we settle it now, either way." Charlie Bojack stepped back, spread his feet apart and spit in Morgan's direction. Morgan saw Billy's fists clench and unclench and he shifted his own position just slightly.

"Pull on me, Bojack. Try me. Like Doc says . . . one less gun won't matter." Doc stepped between them. He glowered at Charlie.

"You don't say nothin' here, Charlie . . . not yet you don't. You'd best remember that."

Now, even from their own position some distance away, the group could hear the rising crescendo of the Apache war dance. Doc looked once more at Morgan. His face was contorted with hatred . . . perhaps even a little fear. The look slowly dissolved to a sneer.

keep low, Morgan . . . I'll be close. No Apache warrior is gonna deprive me o' what's rightful mine. We'll play the hand together . . . for now."

13

No one slept that night. A dozen men, already enemies, were facing what could be their last night on earth. Each knew the horror they faced if they fell into Apache hands. Some had thoughts of spending their last night with a bottle and a woman. Only one carried out his fantasy . . . and for completely different reasons. Billy Frye went to see Doc Henry just after midnight.

"I come to ask for a woman," he said. Doc looked up. He too had thought of Molly, but there was a knot in his stomach and no desire in his groin. "I don't wanna die without havin' one."

"Sumbitch! A Goddam *virgin.*" Doc laughed. "You got balls boy, I'll give you that, yessir . . . you got balls."

"They's a young one out there . . . she's the one I want."

"Shit, boy, take her. Go tell Skeet I said you could take her. Fuck 'er eyeballs out, boy." Doc suddenly turned sullen again. "I was thinkin,' Billy boy . . . I was thinkin' about offerin' them women to

Naschitti. They's nine of 'em. Molly, she screwed me too . . . that's ten." Doc looked up. "You think that fuckin' Apache would take them women an' ride off?"

Doc was asking Billy about something. The very idea amazed Billy, but the suggestion turned his stomach. He knew Doc would do it if he could save his own hide. Billy eyed Doc carefully. Right now, he could kill him. Doc was half drunk, slouched down in a big chair. Billy was fast and he could put a bullet between Doc's eyes in an instant. He considered it. Then he thought of the possibility of Naschitti managing to get at Doc. That, he'd like to see.

"He'll be too fuckin' mad," Billy finally said. He pushed his voice to sound tough and confident. Billy hated his voice. It was changing. It sometimes cracked and went high-pitched on him.

"Yeah, kid, we will. *Sumbitch!* That Goddam Lee Morgan brought this on me . . . you know that, boy? *Lee Fuckin' Morgan.* I'm gonna kill the bastard. I'll wait 'til we git rid o' those Redskins at the front door . . . and then I'm gonna kill the fucker."

"You can beat 'im, Doc . . . you can beat 'im easy."

"Beat him? Shit, boy, I'll blow his fuckin' head off first time I git a chance. I don't owe him nothin' an' I don't give a shit if he's faster'n me. I'm gonna kill 'im."

"I'd sure like to see that," Billy said. "Fact of it is, I'd like to kill the other one . . . that there Trigg."

"Would you now? Sumbitch. By God . . . you can! Charlie wanted him, but by God you can do it, boy, yessir. I'm promotin' you right now. You go on over there and fuck that little whore's eyes out an' tomorrow you can kill that other sumbitch!"

Billy smiled, nodded and hurried away. He felt sick. He fought the nausea. He entered the building where the women were being held. Their fear led them to half cover themselves. Beth was curled up in the corner with her head on Gretchen's lap. Molly got to her feet. Billy placed his finger over his lips and moved toward her.

"I'm with you now," he whispered, "with Morgan. I'm taking Beth out. She'll tell you everything later." Molly frowned. "It's true . . . somehow, it'll all be okay."

Billy led Beth to the privacy of one of the unused buildings. No one paid them any attention. Beth was so happy to see Billy still alive that she chattered on about nothing. Finally, in private, she broke down and wept. Billy let her emotions run their course. That done, he told her everything.

"We've got to hold the Apaches until the army gets here, but I promise you, Beth, no Apache will lay a hand on you. I swear it to you." He didn't bother to tell her how he could make such a promise. In fact, however, he planned to use the dynamite on the building if the Indians broke into the compound. The women would never know what hit them.

"If . . . if the army does come and drive off the Indians, Billy, there's still . . ." She didn't need to finish. Billy nodded. "I'm scared, Billy . . . scared clear inside my bones."

"I was, Beth, but no more. I know now what I got to do, an' Trigg and Mister Morgan, they'll help. It'll be fine." Billy believed what he said but the conviction in his heart was not nearly so strong as the tone of his voice.

They stayed together until nearly four o'clock.

The false sunrise had lightened the eastern sky. Billy walked Beth back to the shed. At least the women would have some hope . . . even about their possible deaths.

Several of Doc's men, working alongside Trigg, had placed dynamite in among the boulders blocking the entrance to the valley. Doc had more dynamite, and Morgan and three other men rode west to the ford in the river. Only here could the Apache cross with ease.

As they rode back toward the camp, the eastern sky was slowly turning pink. Morgan rode a little behind the others and his own thoughts leaped from the Uncompahgre to the quiet valley near Boise. He thought of Idaho, the Spade Bit, and home. He couldn't help wondering what his father would say to him now. Indeed . . . what would Buckskin Frank Leslie do? Morgan knew only one thing for sure, the old man wouldn't have run.

The Butterfield stage, westbound, rumbled into Creede. The driver and the shotgun dropped off the seat and the driver opened the door. A tall, gray-haired man emerged.

"I'm looking for the office of the local army command."

"Down t'other end o' town, mister." The driver cocked his head and stepped back in a moment of wonder and then recognition. "I seed yore pitchur in the *Rocky Mountain News*, mister. Three days ago it w'ar."

"Probably so. I'm Senator Venable."

"Tarnation!" The driver jammed two fingers into his mouth and let go a shrill whistle, which quickly gathered a dozen people around the stage. "I jist brung a Yewnineted States Senator to Creede. This here is Senator Venable." A cheer went up. Venable had recently been pushing lesiglation to approve a railroad spur line into Creede. At that moment, he was one of the most popular men in the territory.

That aside, the Senator was nervous and obviously in a hurry. He made a brief speech, apologized for his brevity, and promised a more formal appearance later. Then he hurried off to the army office.

The recent events in the remote mountain country had made their way to Denver by way of loose-fingered telegraph operators. First there was the missing army gun shipment. Apaches seemed on the warpath. The district commander died of a heart attack, and most recently . . . the reported massacre of more than thirty white men.

"I'm Senator Venable. I'd like to speak to the commanding officer at once. It's a matter of the utmost urgency." The trooper acted quickly and a moment later, Venable was ushered into the office of Brigadier General Brian Utley, late of Fort Carson.

"Senator, sir, I'm honored."

"With due respect, General . . . I'm not paying a social call and I don't have a great deal of time for amenities. Where is the main body of troops you were sent here to command?"

"In the field. Enroute here, sir . . . but still in the field."

"When are they due to arrive?"

"Two days."

"I don't believe we have two days. I have always hesitated to use the power of my office to exert authority directly, but in this instance, general, I intend to make an exception."

"Sir?"

"A Pinkerton agent assigned to my staff was sent here a week ago to determine the progress of my efforts to hunt down and capture a band of gun runners. I received this telegraph cable from him three days ago."

Senator . . . Morgan's fate uncertain. Part of Jared's gang in army custody . . . Jared not among them. 30 of his gang massacred by Naschitti. Jared not among them. Naschitti seeking revenge . . . Army troops in the field. Am riding into valley to continue investigation.

Denton

Senator Venable quickly told General Utley the background and other details of the situation. He asked for a drink, and the General noticed Venable's sudden nervousness and the much more sombre countenance.

"I sent a backup man, one who would keep out of sight . . . to watch Agent Denton and look for Mister Morgan. He too is working for me through the Pinkerton agency. That man is here in Creede. And Agent Denton is dead." Senator Venable swallowed, tears filled his eyes. "He's dead, sir . . . at the hands of my own daughter!"

"My God, Senator . . . are you certain of this?"

"I found a letter from Doc Henry Jared among her things. My daughter, Emilia . . . God, she . . . she has been his lover. He murdered my family . . . my son

. . . my other daughter. My God, how could she . . . how could Emmy do it?"

"Senator Venable, sir, I have 75 men here. They are yours, sir, at once."

The Senator, obviously shaken, struggled to regain his composure. In a few moments he stood up. "We must ride into the Uncompahgre valley . . . into wherever those men are. We have to find Morgan and warn him. My other man, John Myers . . . he's been to the valley. He knows the way."

"I've been getting reports of Apache Indian movement . . . a large number of them."

"Naschitti?"

"I wasn't certain, not until now. We do have many of Jared's men, and the others were killed. There can't be many left. Let me send a trooper from your agent, Senator. Please, you stay here, rest. I'll have my men ready to ride within the hour."

"It will leave Creede undefended, general."

"It's a risk we must take. I only hope that we're not already too late."

The first line of attackers charged the entry trail into Winchester Valley a few minutes after five o'clock. There were no more than a dozen of them, and only two were hit. Trigg was among the five men defending the position. Doc Henry, Billy and Morgan stayed back with five others. Trigg had urged Doc's men, all excellent shots, to hold their fire. He wanted to create the illusion of even a lighter defense than actually existed. The hope was to draw in the Apache, withdraw to a line manned by the others and fire to detonate the dynamite.

The second attack involved nearly thirty warriors,

three quarters of the immediately available force. As planned, Trigg and the others withdrew slowly, firing but not really aiming. Suddenly, most of the Indians were astride the pile of boulders. Trigg and the others scattered and the men behind them cut loose with rifles.

The blast rocked the compound's buildings, shattering window glass and oil lamps. Debris ripped into the cool, morning air, and through the smoke and soot, the bodies of men were hurled like rag dolls to their deaths.

As the dust settled, Trigg and his group moved forward. The surviving Apaches were dazed, confused. Those outside the compound, watching in hypnotic astonishment, all became easy targets. The leader, an eagle-nosed young buck, fell under Doc Henry's sights. He killed him with a shot between the eyes and the others fled.

"Round one," Morgan said to Trigg. Billy tensed as he saw Doc Henry walking toward Morgan. Suddenly Doc laughed.

"We won't need the fuckin' army at this rate. We didn't lose a Goddam man."

"And Naschitti won't be so easy," Morgan replied. "He had a man or two out there somewhere, watching. In a half an hour he'll know what happened. I'd suggest you give those women their clothing and whatever weapons you've got. They may be able to help hold the line. If worse comes to worse . . . we can herd them back inside."

"You don't give no orders here, Morgan . . . remember that."

"Then forget it, Doc. Do as you please." Doc looked menacing. He took a step toward Morgan but Charlie Bojack walked up just at that moment.

"I sent Cully west, Doc, right after we blew the hell out o' them Apaches. Tol' 'im to check the fork at the river. He's comin' in." Charlie was pointing. It was Cully's horse and Cully was riding it, but Morgan frowned. Trigg squinted in the morning sun, focussing on Cully's body bouncing in the saddle.

"He's dead," Morgan shouted. Half a dozen Apaches leaped from the gullies just to the west of the compound. They all had rifles. They were too far away for hand guns. Trigg fired first and one of them dropped. One of Doc's men, a young gunny named Beau, took a shot in the head. Morgan dropped two of the Indians. Cully's horse trotted by and Billy looked up. Cully had five arrows in his back and he'd been scalped!

Three of Doc's men, still near the narrow gorge where the fight had taken place, opened fire. They were flanking the remaining Apaches and dropped two more of them. The last one fled on foot.

"Sumbitches! Run, you bastard, run! Come back and we'll blow you to fuckin' hell!"

"Not at this rate of exchange we won't," Morgan said. "We lost two men."

"Get them women dressed. They's some rifles in the house, an' a shotgun too. You stay with 'em, Charlie, ever' minute. One o' them whores tries somethin' funny, blow her tits off."

Morgan found Doc's order and his tone promising. Doc Henry Jared was scared shitless. Morgan knew if he needed an extra edge with Doc, he had it now.

"Billy, you be the youngest an' prob'ly the best runner. Git on down to the fork. Keep your hair but find out if them Apaches is comin' in yet."

"Okay, Doc." Billy cast a side glance at Morgan. Morgan winked. Billy smiled and trotted off toward the river. The women were dressed and armed with a variety of weapons. Two old Springfield army rifles, three Henry repeaters, a couple of Winchesters. There were two old Remington pistols, a Colt .44 and two shotguns.

"I got a line shack up the side o' that hill yonder. If them Apaches git acrost that river, anybody at that shack would have a good clean shot at some of 'em."

"Agreed," Morgan said. "Why not put Trigg up there, too. Between him and Charlie and the women, they could buy us some time to use that dynamite."

"Yeah . . . yeah," Doc said, reluctantly. "Put the dummy up there too."

A scream! One of Doc's men was running toward them. One of the men from the entryway. He raised his arms, waved, then fell. A lance teetered for a moment and then layed over to one side.

"Jeezus!" Doc pointed. Ten or twelve Apache scrambled through the rocks and began firing. Doc looked helpless.

"Looks about right to me, Trigg," Morgan said. Trigg nodded. Morgan raised his Winchester and followed Trigg's finger along an invisible line-of-sight to a small pile of brush. Beneath it, Trigg had placed half a case of dynamite. Two Indians dropped, Morgan fired. Nothing. "Low, dammit." He aimed, fired again. Pay dirt!

The explosion was ear-shattering. The Apaches were gone. So was another of Doc's men.

"We got nine men left . . . nine," Doc said. He took

off his hat and wiped his forehead with his shirt sleeve. It wasn't that hot. Doc was sweating. He watched as Trigg, Charlie, and the women climbed to their positions. He yelled for the other men to gather 'round. Suddenly, an explosion. Another! *Another!*

"The river," Morgan said.

"Look . . . it's the kid." Billy was running, hard and fast. He was carrying a broken Apache lance. He reached the group and handed Doc the weapon.

"They . . . they blew it. They seemed to know where it was. They . . . they must have been watching us." There was a note wrapped around the lance. Doc removed it and held it out.

> Tomorrow is the day of
> your last sun

"Sumbitch!"

"Naschitti is going to make us sweat it out."

"Not me he ain't, Morgan. There's a back way outa this valley."

"Where is it Doc? Up there?" Morgan was pointing to a hill behind the house, its summit perhaps a mile away. Doc looked. The hill was lined with Apache warriors!

14

Trigg and Morgan bedded down that night near the entry of the valley. Billy volunteered as one of the guards at the building where the women were being kept. Two of the other men went up to the line shack to keep an eye on the western approaches to the compound. Doc Henry ran Charlie Bojack off, early in the evening. He did so on the pretense he wanted to be alone. In fact, he went to an upstairs bedroom about ten o'clock.

"We're gittin' out," he said. Emmy Venable laughed. "I tol' you before, woman . . . don't never laugh at me."

"Getting out? Don't be ridiculous, Doc. I've seen and heard what's going on. How in the hell are we going to get out?"

"You think I'm stupid don't you, woman? You think 'cause you're the fancy pants daughter o' some hifalootin' Senator that you know ever'thing an' I don't know nothin'."

"I didn't say that, Doc."

"You don't have to say nothing'. I know what you

140

think. I seen your kind before . . . Southern mostly, durin' the war. Well, I'm tellin' you, we're gittin out . . . tonight!''

Emmy suddenly realized that Doc Henry was serious. He did have another way out of Winchester Valley. "We're sure to be spotted."

"We go on foot, due east. We got some climbin' to do, but then we come down on the river. I got me a boat hid away down there. We go down river 'til we're south o' Creede. We can get horses and supplies from Luke Halstead."

"Luke Halstead is dead, Doc . . . cut down by Morgan and your man Jess. Didn't you *know* that?"

Doc looked at her. "Sumbitch," he mumbled. He thought for a moment. "No," he finally said, "I didn't know it. I knowed there was a fracas o' some kind, but I didn't know Halstead was in on it. Well, no never mind. We'll take what we need from Luke's daddy. He argues . . . I'll *kill* 'im."

"It still sounds risky to me but it's better than the Apaches laying their hands on us. Besides, the two of us might stand a chance."

"Three, woman . . . they'll be *three* of us."

"Charlie! You're tellin' Charlie Bojack about this?"

"Charlie, hell. We're takin' that Irish whore. Just in case somebody trails us . . . just in case that sumbitch Morgan lives, I want that Irish whore along."

"Damn it, Doc, she's dead weight. She'll slow us down."

"She goes," Doc said. Emmy knew it was useless to argue the point. "Get changed. Nothin' goes with us but money an' guns. I'll go git the whore."

Across the compound, Morgan leaned carelessly back against a boulder. Trigg was rolling a smoke. "How 'bout it, Mahrgan . . . want one?"

"No thanks, Trigg."

"You look to be a man thinkin' about somethin' more than tomorrow marnin.' "

"As a matter of fact, I was. I was thinking what I'd do if I was in Doc Henry's spot."

"You mean run?" Morgan sat up and looked at Trigg with surprise. Trigg smiled. "I was thinkin' the same thing, Mahrgan . . . 'bout an hour back."

"Okay, Irishman, which way?"

"I'm not knowin' the country all that well, Mahrgan, but the bastard don't have a lot of choices does he now?"

"He's got east."

"An' what's over the hill?"

"The Rio Grande . . . flowing south."

"A boat?"

"Why not?"

"Makes sense. Where would he end up?"

"Creede mebbe . . . or South Fork and the Butterfield."

"An' his men?"

"He'll let the Apaches have them, Trigg . . . and us and the women too."

"I know the kind, Mahrgan, I've seen 'em before. Alright then, do we stop him?"

"One of us has to try, don't we?"

"I'm no gun fighter, Mahrgan. A fair hand with a rifle. More than good with the old Sharps . . . but no gun fighter."

"And who stands against the men he leaves here? Billy Frye isn't that good."

"So I go now . . . wait and . . ."

"Without a second thought, Trigg. If you hesitate, Doc will kill you."

"I'll have no trouble with hesitation, Mahrgan. I'd just like to see the bastard hang."

"So would I, Trigg . . . but that doesn't seem too likely." Morgan leaped to his feet when he heard footsteps. Out of the darkness came Billy Frye.

"I told Doc I ought to check the posts. He agreed. The real reason I'm here, Mister Morgan, is . . ." he looked at Trigg. Trigg understood.

"Molly?"

Billy nodded. "He came and got her a few minutes ago."

"He's taking her along."

"I hadn't thought of that," Trigg said. "I can't let that happen."

"You can't stop it, Trigg . . . not without a full-fledged showdown right now, tonight. We're not ready for that."

"I won't let him take her, Mahrgan."

"Trigg! Use your head. He won't hurt her. He wants her for protection."

"And if you're wrong?"

"I'm not, Trigg. Think about it, man. Don't let your feelings slow you down. You do that, you're a dead man."

"You really think Doc's gonna run?"

"Yeah, Billy, I do. So does Trigg, here. You get on back to the others. Keep an eye on them, close. Be ready to make a move in the morning. We're going to try to get the women and make it to the river as well. Trigg, take Doc out. Wait for us . . . with Molly."

Doc took Molly back to the house. She assumed he intended to take her to bed. Minutes after they got there, she was wishing he would. He bound her ankles together and tied her hands behind her back. Then, he gagged her. Emmy walked in, looked down and winced at the pleading look on Molly's face.

"I still think taking her is a mistake."

"You don't run with me to do the thinkin'," Doc said. "You ready?" She nodded. "Then you wait. I'm gonna make a final round o' the compound. Let ever'body see me . . . let 'em think ever'thing's fine. When I git back, we go."

After Emmy was certain that Doc was outside the house, she returned to the bedroom and knelt beside Molly. "Just do as you're told and you won't get hurt. I promise you that . . . you won't." Molly frowned and tried to speak but the effort was futile. "If you don't do what you're told . . . I'll kill you, personally."

Less than fifteen miles from Winchester Valley, Senator Venable was finishing a cup of coffee and lighting a cigar. He offered one to General Utley.

"Thank you, sir. It's not often I'm privy to a really good cigar."

"The late war, General . . . I assume you served."

"I did. I was Lieutenant Utley then. Eastern theatre. Served with Little Mac, Joe Hooker, Burnside and, finally, old Grant himself. How about yourself?"

"No . . . no, General, I wasn't in the war. I was a Congressman then. I was offered a commission and a command . . . from Lincoln himself." The senator smiled. "He was desperate at times."

"I'd wager you'd have made a fine field officer. We had more than our share of a shortage."

"Yes, that we did. I've often pondered the outcome had the South been able to sustain the brilliance they enjoyed in the field."

"We'd be riding out under the Stars and Bars most likely."

"The enemy we're facing now wouldn't have made the distinction, would they?"

"Hardly. The Apache nation has been at war for two hundred years. They fought the Spaniards, then the Mexicans, now us. They're a harsh and determined lot . . . not without just cause either."

"But losing to Manifest Destiny. I was opposed to it," Venable said. "It elevated land thievery to lofty heights, I thought. There should have been another way."

"Hmm! But in another hundred years, the Indians, all of them, will be gone. Wiped from the scene as though they had never been there. It seems as foolish as it does shameful. They have much too offer."

"Naschitti too?" Venable asked.

"Once. No more. Naschitti lives for only one thing," the General said, smiling sadly, "he lives to die."

"And what will tomorrow bring?"

"A nasty fight, the deaths of good men, both white and red. Maybe tomorrow Naschitti will die, maybe not. Either way, he will lose."

"Your plan, General? What is it?"

"We break camp at four o'clock. It is my intent to scout ahead and determine Naschitti's main thrust. We'll wait him out, let him become fully engaged

. . . then we attack."

"How do you know we're even in time?"

"I sent a patrol ahead of the main column, Senator. It left Creede several hours ahead of us. They reported back to me just before suppertime. The Apache have covered every trail in and out of Winchester Valley, but there are hold-outs. I'm afraid I can't tell you just who is among them."

"No matter. Whoever it is, tomorrow's confrontation will bring an end to the troubles in the Uncompahgre."

It was well past two a.m. when Doc finally led Molly and Emmy out the back of his house. They moved along a stand of trees, keeping to the shadows. The night was cloudless, but there was no moon. The scent of pine was strong in the air and a light breeze rustled the leaves of the Aspen.

As Doc had said, the climb from the compound to the east was difficult. In the dark, jagged rocks slashed at bare hands and solid footing was at a premium. Doc forced Molly to climb first, putting Emmy second in line. He toted only his handgun and a Bowie knife; a rifle would have been cumbersome and an added burden.

Twice, Molly nearly fell. Only Emmy's assistance prevented it. Doc cussed at the women, urging them on with subtle threats. It was nearly four when they finally reached the first level of the treacherous mountain.

"Please," Molly said, "let me rest here . . . just for a short time."

"You got five minutes," Doc replied, harshly. "I don't plan to git caught half way up the side o' this hill come daylight."

"How do you know there won't be Indians at the top?" Emmy asked. In fact, Doc didn't know. He'd thought about it but decided it was a risk worth taking. He knew damned well where else they were.

"Won't be no Apaches up there," he finally said, pointing. "Only way to it is from the river, and it looks even tougher from that side."

A few minutes later, the trio had resumed the climb. They were within a hundred yards of the top when they heard the first shots. They were faint and distant. The sky was barely light yet, but they knew Naschitti was beginning his last charge. Emmy stopped and turned toward the firing. She looked forlorn . . . lost. She looked down at Doc Henry Jared and he scowled at her.

The last few feet were pure hell. Molly's palms were torn and bleeding, her clothing shredded, her feet covered with blisters. Emmy too had suffered, but her clothing was more suited to the endeavor. When at last they reached the top, it was daylight. Doc's gun was drawn and he eyed the terrain to the east very carefully. He could see the first rays of the morning sun as they struck the ribbon of water that was the Rio Grande, some two miles distant.

"That shootin' won't last too long," he said. Then, Doc laughed.

By the time Doc and the two women had covered about a mile, a new round of rifle fire began. It sounded closer and it had a dull crack to it that stopped Doc in his tracks. He cocked his head. More shots.

"What is it?" Emmy asked. Molly knew. She smiled.

"It's the army," she said. "Those are Springfields." Then they all heard it. The bugle, sounding the charge.

"Sumbitch!" Doc started running toward the river. He motioned for the women to follow him. Molly hesitated, and Emmy pushed her along. The firing was more intense now, a mixture of weapons. Even a few war whoops could be heard as the Apaches realized they were themselves under attack.

The meadowland spread out before the trio, undulating in gentle waves down to the river. Doc tripped and fell. He rolled once and then came back to his feet. At that moment, the Sharps cracked once and the air was split with its booming discharge. The .50 calibre shell, easily able to down a full-grown bull buffalo, dug up the dirt for six feet just short of Doc's position.

"Trigg," Molly screamed. Emmy struck her and she went down. Emmy was on top of her instantly. At the same moment, Doc looked at the rut in the dirt. A furrow almost as straight as a string. His eyes followed its direction while his right hand went into play. He drew and fired in a single motion. The bullet ricocheted off a tree, pulling some bark with it. He was far short of his intended target.

"Git that whore up here." Emmy had easily won the battle with the exhausted Molly. She had her by the hair and Doc pinned Molly's arm behind her, placing the barrel of his gun to her temple.

"Come out where I can see you, sumbitch. Come out now or I'll blow this whore's head off." Doc looked at the horizon. He was squinting into the rising sun. He didn't like it, but it was Emmy who finally spotted Trigg.

"There, off to the right. There he is." Doc looked. The target was still too distant.

"Let her go, Doc. Send her to me and go on your way."

"Sumbitch! That's your dummy, whore . . . the sumbitch talks."

"Let her go, Doc . . . please." It was Emmy who spoke, and Doc was now showing his true colors. He swung the heavy pistol back and to his right, striking Emmy hard on the temple. She went down in a heap.

"Now you, dummy sumbitch. Toss that Sharps away and walk this way. Keep them hands high, real high. You breathe wrong, dummy, an' the whore dies."

Trigg pondered his options. He'd reloaded the Sharps but it would take time to aim and fire it. It wasn't the light weight Winchester or Henry. He was wearing a handgun, but he hadn't lied about his skill. Trigg was no match for Doc Henry Jared.

"I'm coming," Trigg finally said. He hefted the Sharps high where Doc could see it, then he tossed it aside.

"Don't do it," Molly screamed. "Don't, Sean! He'll kill you!"

"Shawn? That sumbitch is your man?"

"My brother, Doc. For God's sake, don't kill 'im, I'm beggin' you."

Now Trigg had come within range. He stopped.

"You're not much of a man, Jared . . . not much at all. Shoot me, then . . . and Molly there. The other one, too. She's already unconscious. No threat to you. You should be able to handle her with ease."

In a single move, Doc raised the barrel of his gun, brought it down on Molly's head and turned her loose. She dropped to her knees and then collapsed. Doc had his pistol holstered before she hit the ground.

"Now you dummy Irish bastard . . . now tell me I'm no Goddam man." Trigg reached. He'd practiced. He'd learned accuracy. Even some speed. He could have impressed his many fellow soldiers back in Ireland. He looked impressive and might have bluffed his way through a saloon brawl or two in the West. But against Doc Henry Jared, he wasn't even a novice. He never cleared leather. Doc's shot went straight through Patrick Sean Terrence O'Flynn's heart. He blinked once and his lips formed a single word. "Molly," he whispered. Then he fell dead.

As Doc glanced up, he thought he saw movement near the river. He dropped to his knees. There it was again. A hat. Another. Blue.

"Shit! A cavalry patrol." They were checking the river bank for Apaches. He could still hear gunfire back to the west but it was even more distant. The Apaches were running and the cavalry was hard on their asses. "The compound. They'll have it searched by the time I git back."

Doc waited until he could no longer see signs of the army patrol. Both women were still out. In fact, Emmy looked dead. "Too bad," Doc muttered. "I liked your style, Emmy. Liked the way you figgered things. Too fuckin' bad. We'd a' done good, you an' me." Doc got to his feet and trotted back toward his compound in Winchester Valley.

Even as the events by the river were unfolding, Morgan had his hands full. General Utley's troopers had disrupted the main Apache attack and most of the Indians had pulled back, uncertain of the number of troops confronting them. But two dozen or more had gained the compound itself. Morgan, the remaining members of Doc's gang, Billy Frye, and four of the women were holding them at bay from the main house. The other women were taking shifts reloading the weapons. At about six thirty, there was a lull in the fighting.

"By my count, there's still fifteen or so out there. They'll be back."

"Where the fuck is Doc an' that bitch he was with?" Charlie Bojack was beginning to wonder if Doc Henry had run out on him. Morgan, of course, assumed that the woman Charlie was referring so unkindly to was Molly.

"My guess is he ran out on you, Bojack."

"I'm gonna kill you, Morgan . . . even if them fuckin' Apaches git in here. I swear, I'm gonna kill you."

"We can't be fightin' amongst ourselves," Billy said. "Take it easy, Charlie. There's time for that. Hell, they's still five o' us left . . . they's only one o' him."

The Apaches resumed their attack and rendered the exchange academic.

"Now," one of the man yelled, "hit that dynamite case." Seven warriors had gained access to the yard area just west of the house. Their position now afforded them possible entry unless they were stopped. Charlie, Morgan, and Billy all cut loose on the dynamite they'd buried overnight. Three of the warriors died instantly, Morgan and Charlie dropped the others. One of the gang was fatally hit during the fight, along with one of Molly's girls.

The Apaches had suffered all the losses they cared to endure. Only a few had not been driven off by the army, and the accuracy of the fire directed against them, coupled with the open ground they had to cross, had proved devastating. The remainder now fled.

It was one of Doc's men who first realized it. Lefty Hightower saw them riding east. The running battle between Naschitti's main band and the cavalry could still be heard, but it grew more faint with each passing moment. Lefty moved from his upstairs window and carefully edged down to the main floor.

"Can you see 'em?" Billy asked Morgan. Both men were at the windows. Morgan replied that he could not. Lefty caught Charlie's eye, but Gretchen spotted the exchange.

"Look out, Morgan!" Lefty, his gun already drawn, shot and killed Gretchen instantly. Billy darted across the room toward where the rest of the women were located. Morgan went through the window, followed closely by two shots. Both missed. Billy herded all the women through a bedroom window on the ground floor and told them to hide in the woods nearby.

Lefty Hightower, Charlie Bojack, and a man called Petrie remained in the living room. They were trying to pin down Morgan's location. Morgan had taken refuge behind the well in the front yard. The fourth man, Jace Ryker, had watched what Billy Frye did. Ryker now walked onto the back porch. Only Billy stood between Ryker and the women.

Ryker was a gritty-looking sort. He sported a stubble of whiskers where they would grow, but he'd suffered pox as a boy and there were blotches on his face where no hair would grow, making him look all the more sinister. In fact, Jace Ryker was only a little older than Billy. He was alleged to have once ridden with the James boys on a bank holdup, and a wanted poster on him told of his murder of a sheriff somewhere in Oklahoma Territory. The other story about him focused on his lightning fast draw.

He wore a Colt .45 with an Ebony covered butt . . . an unusual and attractive weapon. It was tied to his right leg about midway between his waist and his knee. When he positioned himself to draw it, he didn't take the usual wide-legged stance. Rather, he put most of his weight on his left leg and extended his right leg forward just a bit. The butt of the Colt then protruded from his thigh in a position affording him the fast draw for which he was reputed.

"I figgered you fer a fuckin' traitor, Frye. Figgered it a long time back." Ryker grinned and licked his lips. "One thing you got is good taste in women. That young one, that there Beth." Ryker raised his eyebrows and nodded his head slightly. "Soft pussy, I'll bet. I figger to have it, Frye . . . jist as soon as I kill you."

"You got it wrong, Ryker. I was herdin' them women out o' here 'til we could take out Morgan. Hell, Ryker, you can have that young one," Billy forced a half laugh. "She ain't bad."

"You're a lyin' bastard, Frye. All you had to do was throw down on them women and we'd 'a' had them an' Morgan. Now pull on me, Frye, 'cause if you don't . . . I'm gonna pull on you." Ryker grinned again. "You're a dead bastard either way."

Billy Frye had come of age. There was no more distance. Shooting an Indian or any man from twenty or fifty or a hundred yards was a whole lot different than eye-to-eye. His throat went dry and he couldn't find the spit to swallow. There was only silence save for the faint popping of rifles far to the west.

Billy's mind was reeling with self portraits of his long hours of practice. Draw and fire . . . draw and fire. A split second later, the image vanished and was replaced by Morgan's words. Now Billy Frye asked himself the question. "Can I kill a man in a gun fight?" His answer was less than fifteen feet away from him.

Charlie Bojack stepped through the back door. "What the fuck is goin' on?"

"Frye here decided to switch sides, Charlie. He run them girls up the hill to hide an' then tried to lie his way out. He's mine, Charlie; you an' the others keep Morgan tied down."

Charlie looked at Billy. Billy's face was all the confirmation he needed. "Yeah, Jace . . . good idea. Take the kid out." Charlie turned and re-entered the house. It bothered Billy. He didn't know if it was a display of confidence in Ryker or a show of contempt for Billy. His mind flashed back to Morgan's near shoot-out with Doc Henry.

"You're makin' the bet, Ryker . . . an' I'm callin' you. Show your hand."

Ryker slapped leather. The pretty little Colt fairly flew from the holster and spit lead twice. Ryker's eyes had widened in surprise even as he began the move. He could already see the twin black dots that were the barrels of Billy's guns. Billy fired one shot from each. Ryker's bullets went wide and high. Billy's struck the upper right chest and the belly. Ryker teetered for a moment, managed one foot forward in a vain effort to deny the truth, grimaced in a moment of pain, and fell dead.

Billy darted around the corner of the house to near the front. "Morgan . . . Ryker's dead. I gunned him. The women are hidden in the trees." Billy heard the front door of the house open.

"Morgan, you sonuvabitch . . . show yourself." Lefty Hightower stepped out and stood at Charlie's right. In a moment they were joined by the man called Petrie. "It's three to two," Charlie said, "but you're supposed to be so fuckin' good that won't make no never mind . . . will it, Morgan?"

Morgan stood up. "Get the women, Billy, and get out of here."

"Not yet, Mister Morgan," Billy said. He walked across the yard and positioned himself on the opposite side of the well from Morgan. They were about twenty five feet from the house. The trio of men on the porch came off it and stood in the yard.

"Hightower's fast," Morgan said, "but he bends his knees just before he shoots. It costs him time. I'll take Bojack. I can't tell you about Petrie."

"I've seen 'im," Billy said. "He's not as good as Ryker."

Billy Frye had come from a two-gun-toting loud-mouth to a subdued and skilled gunman almost in the blink of an eye. Petrie went for Billy. Petrie's eyes were glued to Billy's right hand gun. It was logical; Petrie was on Charlie's left and in the line of fire for Billy's right hand. Billy was faster, and he proved it. He was also smarter! He drew both weapons but crossed them in front of him as he fired.

Petrie died instantly. Lefty Hightower got off a shot which Billy felt as it grazed his neck like the sting of a wasp. Lefty took Billy's shot in the leg, staggered, and caught a second shot that killed him. It too came from one of Billy's guns. Even later, he could not recall which one he'd fired twice.

Morgan, for his own protection and to buy Billy another fraction of a second, concentrated on Charlie Bojack. Charlie's arm seemed almost disconnected from the rest of his body when he drew. It was so fast as to make a man wonder if his brain could work that fast. Morgan's hat flew from his head, somersaulting through the air. There was a hole, dead center just above the wide band.

Morgan's own right hand almost tingled from the tension in every nerve ending. There was no feeling Morgan had ever experienced that was exactly like it. He'd often thought the feeling came from a momentary visit by Death itself . . . but if so, Death always passed Lee Morgan by. Morgan's hand and arm and the gun they manipulated all ended up three or four inches lower than that of any other man there. The bullet he fired ended up in the target just an inch or two higher. It defied explanation but the results were obvious. Charlie Bojack died two quickly to show any response. He fell forward, stiff as a board, still looking straight ahead. The impact flattened his nose.

"How bad you hit?" Morgan asked. Billy wondered how Morgan could know. Even Billy wasn't yet certain. He touched the wound.

"Scraped me, that's all."

"You lost time crossing your guns. Against better men, you'd be dead."

"I'll remember, Morgan."

Morgan smiled. "Yeah, Billy, do that. But you're good, damn good."

"What now?"

"I'll round up enough horses for everybody. You get the women down here." Morgan cocked his head. There was no more distant firing . . . only the gentle whistle of the breeze through the pines.

"It's over, Mister Morgan." Morgan looked at Billy, but he said nothing. He knew it wasn't over. He'd come for Doc Henry and he hadn't got him yet.

Morgan found the roan just where he'd left him. Two other animals were nearby, but no others could be seen. He decided, if worse came to worse, he'd have Billy stay with the women and he'd make contact with the army. He led the mounts back to the house. Billy was sitting on the porch steps, hat in hand and staring at the ground.

"What is it, Billy?" Billy looked up. Morgan could see the glisten of moisture in Billy's eyes.

"The women, Mister Morgan. It's all my fault . . . they're *gone*!"

"Jared," Morgan said to himself. "He doubled back."

"What'd you say?" Billy got to his feet. He walked over and handed Morgan the note he'd found stuck to a tree with a Bowie knife.

You follow . . . they're dead.

"It's not your fault, Billy. You did the right thing."

"I want 'im, Mister Morgan . . . I want 'im bad."

Morgan nodded. "Yeah, Billy, but you're at the back of the line. Ride out of here and find the army. Tell them what's happened and tell them about the women."

"I want to go with you."

"Don't argue, Billy. Just do what I tell you to. Don't make me force it." Billy saw Morgan's eyes and the set of his jaw. He knew he'd lose this one. He nodded passively.

Morgan rode to the edge of the tree line, stopped, and turned back. Billy was riding west. Morgan looked at the compound and thought how serene it looked . . . how pleasant now. Then something gripped at his innards. It was the old feeling of hatred. The feeling that went back to Harvey Logan and the death of his father. Out there somewhere was Morgan's Harvey Logan . . . in the body of Doc Henry Jared.

15

The rain was incessant. It didn't fall . . . it was driven. Drops the size of a man's thumb, and cold. Billy Frye hunkered down even lower in his saddle. No one had spoken for the last five miles. The soldiers were weary and dejected, the column a morbid snake of men crawling along a mountain trail, toting their own dead.

General Utley had begun his campaign with considerable zeal and no small measure of success. Surprise was his ally and Naschitti was clearly on the defense. Perhaps that was Utley's mistake. He simply forgot that the Indian, never mind the tribe, had always fought on the defense. Naschitti was brilliant in his withdrawal from Winchester Valley. He ordered his warriors to split up and flee in apparent terror of the sudden appearance of the Blue Coats.

In fact, Naschitti had carefully planned his movements, drawing General Utley's main force still deeper into the Uncompahgre. He used brilliant hit and run tactics along the way until, finally, his main force had gathered again. Their counter attack decimated Utley's command and the General himself sustained a serious wound. But Naschitti also knew when his own time had run out. He knew there were more soldiers . . . and he didn't know where. It was the only thing that saved Utley's command from being wiped out.

Billy caught up with the returning force just as it broke the trail north of Slumgullion pass. General Utley was too feverish even to accept Billy's report. It made no difference anyway. He'd simply ride with them back to Creede. The rain began on the mountain top and grew increasingly worse.

Senator Venable had argued to try and force entry into the valley where Doc Henry had been holed up. Soon, even he realized the effort would be futile. Reluctantly, with a small detachment to accompany him and, he hoped, lead Yates back into the fight, the Senator headed back to Creede.

As Billy rode along in silence, he couldn't keep his imagination from conjuring up the worst possible scenarios. They included Doc Henry's cold-blooded murder of all the women, or his rape of Beth and their abandonment in the high country. Billy knew that Lee Morgan wouldn't give up, but that was little consolation where the safety of the women was concerned.

Morgan was frustrated. The country over which Doc Henry had chosen to go was not suited to riding a horse. Morgan led the roan through some rugged terrain and could only hope the animal wouldn't slip, go crippled on him, or simply bolt from Morgan's almost impossible demands.

Morgan knew only that Doc Henry had been

working, slowly, back to the west. Morgan's knowledge of the Uncompahgre wasn't sufficient to draw any conclusions about an ultimate destination. Four days had passed since the shoot-out in the valley, and Morgan's only thread of encouragement had come from the women. One of them, maybe Beth, had been marking a trail. A small bit of cloth here, a piece of silk or satin there. Someone lived, someone besides Doc Henry.

Morgan, in spite of the loosely marked trail, harbored grave concerns for the lives of the women. There was no lack of water in the high country, but food was another matter. Morgan had seen no smoke; Doc Henry would never allow a fire. He could feel the drain on his own body from a restricted diet of jerky and hard tack. The open meadow country, and there were many miles of it, did nothing to aid Morgan's efforts. Doc Henry kept to the high country, and Morgan dared not risk losing the meager trail someone was leaving.

Shortly after sunup on the morning of his fifth day out, Morgan spotted a man! He too was seen, but the man made no move to run or confront Morgan. He simply rode toward him, slowly. They met at a crystal clear stream that cut a path through the meadowland.

"Jehosophat! You look nigh on to daid." The man slipped off his horse. He was a giant and made more so by a double layer of clothing . . . buckskin and bear hide. "I be called Stoner."

"Morgan . . . Lee Morgan. I'm trailing a man and several women." Stoner spat a wad some twenty feet and wiped his whiskers. His shirt sleeve was dark brown where he'd done the same thing untold times in the past.

'Them wimmin fo'k looked mighty sorrowful.''

"You saw them? When? Where?"

"It w'ar two day back. Four they wuz . . . an' a surly feller herdin' 'em up trail.''

"Damn. Four is all?"

"Yep. I give 'em som b'ar meat . . . fresh kilt that mornin'.''

The grizzly old mountain man then went to fishing through his many pockets. He finally grinned, exposing short, dingy teeth.

"One o' them wimmin, she sez if'n I meet anybody to be sure an' give 'em this.'' Morgan took the crumpled paper. The note was short, written with a burned stick.

> Molly alive—no here.
> Only four. Silverton.
>
> Beth

Morgan suddenly felt a new surge of hope. Molly must have slipped away. Or had she been abandoned? Not likely, he decided. Beth! Morgan wished he could get word to Billy. He looked up. Maybe he could.

"Where you bound for, Stoner?"

"Wh'ar ever that ol' horse'll carry me a'fore the snow flies.''

"Creede," Morgan said. He pulled out a hundred dollar bill. "You ride to Creede for me. Deliver a message to the army and to a young buck named Billy Frye. I'll write the words so you won't have to remember them. Do that, Stoner, and you can winter it out in Creede . . . high livin'. This hundred's yours now . . . I'll have to trust you to that much. Do what I ask and there'll be two hundred more in it. You've got my word."

"Had me a whole poke full o' hunnert dollar bills oncest. Struck gold up in South Park." The old man reared back his head and let out a war whoop followed by stacatto laughter. "Lost every penny of it to a bunko steerer in a Denver saloon."

"Sorry," Morgan said.

"Sorry? No need to be feelin' sorry, sonny." Stoner once again began rummaging through his pockets and talking at the same time. "I waited fer that feller fer two month er more. He final come ridin' along Cherry crik one night. I cut his gizzard out." Morgan frowned. He needed the old man's cooperation, but he had no time for tall tales. Stoner's face lit up. "Here 'tis." He held up a short length of thong leather. "Took his ear too." The leathery ear dangled from the rawhide.

"I need your help, Stoner . . . I mean those women do. The man they were with was Doc Henry Jared. You ever hear of him?"

"Nope," Stoner said without hesitation. "Don't palaver much with city fo'k . . . don't like cities. Don't like Creede." He shifted the chew in his cheek, lined his sight on a columbine and it disappeared beneath a dark brown blob. "Don't like it none, but I'll do it for ya. Been a spell sincest I wintered indoors."

Morgan quickly penned a note to the commanding officer at Creede and a separate one to Billy Frye. He wasn't sure who was in command by now, but he urged them to return to the compound and began a search for Molly and possibly others. He told Billy to meet him in Silverton.

Morgan sat atop the roan and watched until the old mountain man reached the end of the valley. Stoner stopped, turned back and waved and then headed south. He was going to help.

Two of the women were too weak to continue. Doc Henry finally yielded to Beth's pleadings that they stop for the night. He had managed to snare a rabbit, and Beth along with a girl named Alicia set about to cook it. The wind was out of the east, coming down from one of the nearby high peaks. Doc felt safe that no one behind him would see smoke. The other women fell asleep quickly, and Doc leaned back against a rock some distance from the fire.

"Beth, keep working," Alicia said, "but listen." Beth nodded. "We're traveling west . . . almost due west now. We've been traveling this way for five days. We're very close to the roads. Very close."

"What road?"

"It runs north and south between Ouray and Silverton where Doc Henry said he was going. I worked in Ouray once . . . a mining camp there. I traveled the road south. It went down to Silverton over a high mountain pass. We're real close to it, Beth."

"How can you be sure, Alicia? My God, we're in the middle of the mountains."

"Look up, Beth . . . due west." Beth did. What she saw was one peak with a little snow at its summit and a reddish tinge along its slopes.

"I don't see nothin' but that there funny lookin'

red mountain."

"That's it, Beth . . . Red Mountain. That's the pass I went over between Ouray and Silverton. We look to be a little north of it. If we go west, through that flat country, we'll come out on the trail. There's always minin' equipment goin' back an' forth . . . men too, ever'day between Ouray and Silverton."

Beth's heart pounded hard. If Alicia was right, they had only a few more hours to live. Perhaps Doc agreed to stop here only so that he might kill them. It couldn't be more than a few hours walk to that road. He wouldn't need them anymore, and he certainly didn't intend that they should live to tell their story.

"Alicia, in the mornin' I want you to go tell Doc you're makin' a trip into the woods . . . you know, to pee or somethin.' "

"You mean . . . ." Alicia's eyes got big. "Try somethin'?"

"What choice we got? While you're doin' that, I'll git Doc over to one o' the other girls . . . tell him I think she's daid and ask him to look. 'Stead o' peein', you be waitin'. Git a rock or tree branch, anythin'. If we don't git now, he'll kill us . . . ever' one of us."

"Where's that fuckin' rabbit?"

"Comin', Doc, it's comin'."

Even the women who were asleep were grateful for having been awakened. The rabbit tasted like beef steak, but one of the sickest women couldn't keep it down, and within an hour after she'd eaten, she was sicker than ever.

Just after dark, Doc set about to tying them up as he had done each night. The second one was the sick girl. Beth was nearby and heard a slight groan. Then, with the last dying rays of the sun, she caught the gleam of light off the knife blade!

Doc moved to Alicia next. She pulled back as he squeezed one of her tits and then laughed. He slapped her and she began to sob, softly. He stood up, legs spread, and said, "Think I'll have myself a little treat tonight, after that there rabbit dinner."

Beth had never moved so quickly. She cleared the distance to where Doc was standing in four leaps. He heard her steps and turned, but she was already in position. She kicked, hard. The heavy boot struck home. Doc howled and doubled over in pain. She grabbed for his gun. He swatted at her, but he'd dropped to his knees. She aimed the Colt at his head and pulled the trigger. The hammer dropped onto an empty chamber! They were all empty. Doc had taken no chances.

He was still holding his balls with one hand, but he'd managed to get back on his feet. He never heard Alicia behind him with the branch. It caught the back of his head and he went down face first. It was a solid blow, but lacked force. Doc groaned again, shaking his head.

"Run, Beth . . . run now." Alicia already was fleeing, and Beth was confused. One girl was still alive and it was nearly dark. Doc wasn't dead and she had no way to kill him. She swung the Colt but the butt missed its mark, catching Doc on the back of the neck. He went down again and Beth turned and ran.

Morgan had gotten some beans and dried bear meat from Stoner. The old man also poured a

healthy amount of whisky into Morgan's canteen.
This night, Morgan wouldn't camp. Trail or no trail,
he knew his ultimate destination and he figured to
close the gap between him and his prey. He ate the
beans as the big roan walked easy through the
meadow. He washed down the bear meat with
whisky and felt a new strength. By dark, Morgan
was riding steady toward the darkening sky to the
west. His landmark was the silhouette of Red
Mountain pass.

It was well after sunup when Morgan again found
a tiny piece of cloth. Beth was a smart girl. She
always marked the trees to the right and poked a
hole through the cloth if there was no change in
direction. Where there was a direction change, she
would knot the cloth. Morgan's own tracking skills
more than made up the deficits.

At mid-morning, Morgan rode into the camp. He
found rabbit bones, a still warm fire bed, and two
dead girls. He felt a moment of guilt when he
realized he was relieved that neither of them was
Beth Frye. He didn't tarry long—only long enough
to bury the girls in shallow graves.

He crossed Animas creek near noon and he knew
it was less than five miles to the base of Red
Mountain. He'd found no more cloth and no tracks.
He wasn't sure of his direction from Silverton, but
he was aware of the mining road not too far away.
His fear now was that he would be too late to save
Beth and one other girl, whoever she was.

"Morgan? Oh my God . . . Mister Morgan!" He
looked toward a small pond formed from the creek's
recent overflow and there stood Beth Frye.

"Where's Doc?" Morgan's Colt was already out.

He'd shoot on sight. She shook her head.

"He went south . . . we saw him. We were scared to death he'd find us again. We hit him and ran away last night after he killed Mary."

"He on foot?" Beth nodded. "How long ago did he pass?"

"Two hours, mebbe three. I'm not sure. Alicia . . . I think her leg's broke."

Beth was right. Doc Henry would have to wait, and so would Morgan. He put both women on the big roan and they set out for the road. At least tonight they'd bed down inside. They were headed for Ouray.

The Elk Horn Palace was a sham. The facade would have done any street in New York City proud. Once you walked through the bat wings, it ended. Still, it was inside. The sheets were clean. Yellowed with stains, but clean. Besides, there wasn't anything else in Ouray, Colorado.

Alicia had a room for the night in the sawbone's house, where the doc had set her leg. Morgan got himself and Beth adjoining rooms. After he'd treated her to a fine dinner, he saw to it she got bedded down. He slipped out and wandered into the bar.

"You drinkin', mister . . . or just takin' up space?"

"I'm looking for the sheriff."

"You'll have a long wait mister. Ain't no sheriff hereabouts."

"There's the territorial marshal," an attractive young girl said. Morgan looked at her and she smiled . . . a come-on smile. He smiled back, but he wasn't interested.

"Where might I find him?"

"Don't know for sure. If he didn't ride down south, he'll be in his office, I reckon. It's down at the end o' the street." Morgan nodded his appreciation.

Halfway there, he saw the flicker of a lamp in the office window. He picked up his pace and entered without knocking. The marshal was a big round-shouldered man with thick gray hair. He was engaged in paperwork and didn't look up.

"What can I do for you?"

"I'm Lee Morgan, marshal." The big man shoved his chair back quickly and got to his feet. He was eyeing Morgan's gun. "I'm not lookin' for trouble. I came for your help."

"I got a dodger on you, Morgan."

"Probably. Mebbe two." He handed the marshal his letter from Senator Venable. The marshal shoved some papers back and forth looking for his glasses. He finally found them, and took a closer look at the young muscular man he'd heard about before.

"Lee Morgan, eh?" The marshal read the letter and handed it back. "I'm Ephram Banner." Morgan tilted his head. He was trying to remember where he'd heard the name before. "I knew your daddy."

"Then that's why the name sticks."

"In your craw, mebbe . . . that right?"

"No."

"Well, mebbe it should." Banner walked to a dusty old chest in the corner. It was a roll-top and he blew away some of the grime before he opened it. Inside, in three neat stacks, each a foot thick, there were wanted posters. Banner fingered through the first stack until he reached the halfway point. He lifted the top half and slipped a yellowed sheet out. It nearly tore in two. He turned and handed it to Morgan. It offered a $1.,500 reward for Buckskin Frank Leslie, alias Lee Williams, alias Fred Lee.

Morgan handed the poster back. "He's dead, marshal."

"I heard that. Who backshot him?"

"Nobody. Harvey Logan got him."

"Fair draw?" Morgan nodded. "Then Logan's dead too."

"He is."

"And you're claimin' to be a Pinkerton man."

"I'm a Pinkerton man at the request of Senator Venable . . . that's all."

"Your daddy never asked me for help." He grinned. "I chased him over most o' three states. Felt lucky I never caught up to him when it mattered."

"But you did catch up to him."

"Dodge City. Youngster named Toby Jacobs got shot during a bank robbery. The Tyler brothers, Kiley Haddock from down Missouri way, and little John Ringo. Ringo skedaddled clear out o' Kansas. Drifted south. Me'n your daddy an' Morgan Earp an' Doc Holliday went after 'em. We got 'em. Now Kiley, he was smooth, fast. A right fine gun hand. Frank Leslie beat him clean and drilled a hole through his right elbow. Shattered it." The marshal looked down at Morgan's rig. "That the Bisley?"

"Yeah."

"I never drew against him." Banner laughed. It was a soft laugh, deep from his belly. It reminded Morgan of Frank Leslie's laugh.

"Well, I know Senator Venable sure. If that

letter's on the up an' up, then you've got my help. If
it's a scam, son . . . I'll kill you. Want some coffee?"
Morgan nodded. Banner poured them both a cup
and they both sat down. "Alright, son, tell me your
story."

Marshal Banner took in every word without
expression until Morgan finished. Then Banner
leaned forward. "Doc Henry Jared has never come
this far west. We don't want him here, and folks
aren't going to appreciate the Pinkertons taking on
somethin' they can't finish." Morgan got to his feet.
"You goin' somewhere?"

"Back to my room, marshal. I'm dead ass tired.
As far as folks are concerned, we'd best get Doc
Henry quick. No need for them to know anything if
we do the job."

"You're not as smooth as your daddy was."

"Nor as patient," Morgan said.

"Mind if I walk with you? Haven't made my
rounds anyway."

"You're welcome."

They were half way back to the Elk Horn Palace
before the marshal spoke again. "Any idea why
Jared would go to Silverton?"

"Only one. Doc's brother rode back south to help
him with his Apache deal. Johnny's dead, but I
found out later that he didn't ride south alone. He
had three men with him and he left them in Silverton to wait for him. He'd told Doc about it in a letter
several months ago."

"And these three men?"

"Largo Johnson, Quint Yokley, and Charlie
Hawks." Marshal Banner stopped dead in his

tracks.

"Shootists don't come worse than them three, Morgan."

"Damn few I ever heard of do."

"I don't know a man this side o' the divide that'll ride against the likes o' them."

"I know three, marshal."

"Name 'em."

"Banner, Morgan, and Frye . . . Billy Frye."

"I'm law an' they don't scare me none an' you say you're workin' for Pinkerton an' that makes you law. I'll take your word on this fella Frye. The odds are still wrong."

"Four to three. I've faced worse."

"You've faced worse numbers mebbe . . . but these odds, Morgan, these are like your daddy's with Harvey Logan."

Morgan looked puzzled. "Odds? How so?"

"They may be even, boy, and that means no winners . . . just seven dead men."

Morgan didn't know what time it was, he only knew that it was still dark, he was still tired, and there was someone in his room.

"Morgan," came the voice . . . low, soft, frightened. "It's Beth." He fumbled and found a match. He lit it. She was wearing one of his shirts and nothing else.

"Couldn't sleep?"

"No. An' . . . an' I'm scared Morgan."

"Don't be. Tomorrow we'll get out of here and you'll get back to Creede." Morgan had been thinking about what he'd told Banner, about the men who'd stand against Doc. "You'll be back with your brother. I told him to meet me in Silverton. If he's not there yet, I'll send you on and send him back to you when he shows up." Beth sat down on the edge of the bed, then she learned over and layed her head on Morgan's bare chest.

"I need to forget for awhile," she said. "Will you help me?" She raised her head and looked into Morgan's face. He knew what she meant. He didn't think he could do it. Not even if he felt like it and, at that moment, he didn't.

"It might complicate things even more."

"How Morgan? Tomorrow we'll split up. Maybe I won't ever see you ag'in." Beth stood up, removed the shirt and Morgan realized she wasn't really a little girl. Her breasts were full, round, and tipped with large, perpetually hard nipples. Beth was fully matured physically and old enough to make her own decisions.

"Love me, Morgan . . . please." She moved to the bed and slipped over his body. She was warm and smelled like a woman should smell. She kissed him and her tongue darted into his mouth. Morgan began to respond. His hands found the fullness of her tits and he kneaded them gently. She raised up and he continued his caresses. She turned around and bent from the waist, lowering herself until she could close her lips around the head of Morgan's already hardened cock.

She sucked greedily at his shaft and Morgan responded with his own tongue. He teased at first and then found his desires too demanding for delay. He licked furiously at her pussy until it was soaked with a combination of his saliva and her juices.

Suddenly Beth got up, rolled to the bed beside him

and spread her legs. Morgan moved on top of her and entered, slowly, carefully. She had experienced a man before, but he felt a tightness around his prick which he had not known for a long time. She contracted her vaginal muscles and increased the sensation as Morgan began to pump. It was slow at first but increased with each stroke.

They kissed and Beth squealed as every nerve ending in her body responded to his efforts. She had been fucked by a boy, a 17 year old boy. She loved him and he was leaving with his family for California. It was their last time together. She had never regetted it but it had left a smouldering within her which Morgan was now fanning into a full flame.

Beth's body heaved and she closed her arms around his neck, digging her fingernails into his back and shoulders. Morgan was near his climax, he moaned.

"God, Beth. God, you're nice . . . young . . . " His sperm burst forth like a broken water pipe. Beth strained and contracted her muscles so that she might join him. She succeeded and they writhed in those precious few seconds when a man and woman truly become one.

16

Butterfield didn't run stages into that part of Colorado. Instead, Beth was put aboard the Montrose-Durango line. It did make a stop in Silverton, but Beth wouldn't even get off. At Durango, she'd wait for the eastbound Butterfield.

She and Morgan had exchanged little talk that morning but she kissed him as they parted. He thought back to the night before and realized that his own needs had been as great as Beth's. He watched the big Concord coach until it was out of sight and then he walked to the marshal's office.

"This is Ole Swenson," Banner said. "He keeps an eye on things when I'm not around." Ole and Morgan shook hands but said nothing. "I'm ready, Morgan." Banner looked up as he put a final item or two in his saddle bags. "I give Ole here an official swearin' in this mornin'. Mayor was witness, an' I turned in a letter of recommendation on Ole."

"Sounds pretty final to me."

"It was, Morgan. How about you? You settled your affairs?"

"I've got none to settle."

"I recollect hearin' somewhere that ol' Buckskin Frank had himself a ranch." Banner looked at Morgan. "Didn't he leave it to you or was that just a story?"

"There was a ranch. The Spade Bit. Idaho. I sold it," Banner detected there was more to it than that but he didn't push the issue.

"Ole, take care o' yourself . . . an' take care o' Ouray for me."

"You'll be back, marshal," Ole said, smiling.

"Mebbe, mebbe not."

It was 23 miles from Ouray to Silverton. A third of it was up one side and down the other on Red Mountain pass. The base of the 11,000 foot peak was very near before either man spoke again.

"You scared, Morgan?" Banner looked at him for an answer.

"I don't know. Most men that I've heard about who were scared ran away. I've never run away." After he'd said that, Morgan wondered if keeping ahead of Harvey Logan and leading Logan back to where he and Frank Leslie shot it out was running. Maybe it was.

"There's a lot o' ways to be scared. Dyin' scares some men."

"You?"

Banner smiled. "I've already lived longer than most in my business. I looked at myself in the mirror this morning and thought about you and decided we're the last o' the lot."

"Meaning?"

"Me . . . an old timer. A man raised up like your daddy was. You, a gun fighter with fewer men to fight and civilization telling you not to. It's not the way anymore . . . not in most places anyways."

"You saying we're out of place?"

"Yeah," Banner agreed, nodding. "Yeah, I guess that's what I'd call us."

"But that civilization you talked about, Marshal . . . it's people. They want to move west, to build and grow and multiply. They can't quite do it yet because of men like Doc Henry. We may be the last, but we've still got a place."

They rode over Red Mountain, pausing only to eat. They eyed the sluice piles and the rotting timbers of long-abandoned mines. The northbound stage and a half a dozen freight wagons passed them. This was civilization and it expected to be left alone to get on with itself. Thousands of men, women, and children trying to scratch out a new life for themselves and their families yet unborn. Between them and men like Doc Henry, there was a handful of dedicated lawmen. At that moment, Lee Morgan was one of them.

Silverton was not Ouray or anything like it. Half a dozen narrow, muddy streets were lined with wooden buildings. The people, shoulder to shoulder as they went about their business, were a mixture of the old and new that Banner and Morgan had spoken about.

Women in Eastern finery, the wives of those who had already made the mountain yield its hidden wealth, mingled with the saloon girls and plain pioneer stock. Men in broadcloth suits and sporting plug hats rubbed elbows with grimy miners and buckskin clad mountain men. Kids rolled hoops through the streets with sticks. The bunco steerers, tin horns and flim-flam men who often made a bigger fortune than those they bilked were as easy to spot as the camp followers.

Banner rode to the middle of town and reined up in front of a small, rickety-looking wooden building. Morgan could see the faded letters on an old sign above the door.

Assay Office

"Sheriff's office," Banner said, as he dismounted.

"You didn't mention a sheriff."

"No need. He won't fight."

Morgan climbed down, secured the reins to the hitching post, and walked around in front of Banner. "We're short one man," he said. "If Billy Frye shows up, I'm sending him back. He's got a family to care for."

"Good idea, Morgan. I figured I'd mention it to you later, if you didn't think of it yourself." Morgan shook his head. Banner was more like Frank Leslie than Morgan had realized.

"If this fella won't fight, why bother with him?"

"Law, Morgan. Rules and regulations, paperwork. It's all part of this . . . civilization. Funny a little. Law says you kill a man, you have to write down somewhere who he was and why you did it."

The sheriff was closer to Banner's age than to Morgan's. He was a small stocky man with deep blue eyes. They were his most noticable feature.

"Howdy, Banner."

"Josh. This is Lee Morgan . . . Pinkerton man. We've come down to make an arrest," Banner paused, glanced at Morgan and then took a deep breath, "there's going to be trouble . . . big trouble."

"Yep. I figgered it right. Three gunmen rode in a mite ago. Still here. I got paper on two of 'em . . . stacks of it."

"There'll be four. Doc Henry Jared is comin' to your town, Josh."

"Already has. The four of 'em set playin' poker last night down to the Hampton House."

"Any trouble?"

"Not a lick or a spit. Whole bunch been behavin' like kids in Sunday school."

"You got a deputy?"

"Not 'ny more. Quit on me after a bunch o' drovers come through town. Skeered clean out o' Silverton."

"Anybody else in town of meanin'?"

"Yep, they is, Banner, now that you bring it up. Colorado Charley Utter."

"He rode with Hickok," Morgan said. "I've heard his name for years."

"That's him," Josh said, beaming now. "First time I met 'im he was with ol' Bill. They come up from Denver er sum such. Bill, he gambled most of a week. Run a tin horn out an' him an' Charlie faced down the Butcher boys. 'Member them, Banner?" The marshal nodded and smiled. "Meaner'n a kicked hound they was, but turnt plumb to jelly when they found out who they was facin'." Josh had been sacking up a few personal items. He was finished now, and finished talking. "Hope I see ya walk through your office door in a few days, Banner . . . but if'n not, been pleasurable knowin' ya." He turned to Morgan. "You too, son."

"Let's get a room," Banner said. "Get the lay of things. Tomorrow or maybe tonight yet, we'll go talk to Colorado Charlie."

"I gather you don't plan to confront Doc right away."

"You said you wanted help from me, Morgan. I'm givin' it."

"If Doc spots me, there'll be no waiting."

"Can you take him?" Morgan nodded. "Then it'll be three to two, won't it?"

They were just entering the Mother Lode hotel when Josh Stalcup rode by headed for Ouray. Banner smiled. It was a smile of sympathy and accompanied by the thought that he, one day soon, might do the same thing in reverse. "He was a hell of a lawman once."

"I couldn't wear a badge and do that," Morgan said.

Banner pushed the door open, hard. There was some contempt in his tone when he said, "You couldn't wear a badge at all, Morgan. You're out o' the wrong bolt o' cloth."

The two men ate an early dinner and returned to their room. Banner stripped off his rig and shirt and stretched out on the bed.

"Wake me up about six o'clock," he said.

"I'd like to get on with this, marshal . . . one way or another." Banner pulled his hat down over his eyes. "Go ahead," he said. "If you have it done by six, lemme sleep another hour."

Morgan was too restless to sleep. He quietly slipped out about thirty minutes later, convinced that Banner knew he went. He walked most of a block in both directions and finally entered one of

Silverton's less conspicuous saloons. He sipped a beer and watched the comings and goings out on the street. It was Friday and the whole town would be different after sundown.

Morgan knew he had to do something. He left the saloon and made his way to the stage station. The telegraph office was there, too, and he sent a telegraph cable to the army office in Creede. It informed them to tell Billy Frye to stay put if he hadn't already left. Morgan knew that it was likely Billy would still be in Creede. Old Stoner, the mountain man, didn't move that fast.

That done, Morgan returned to the room. It was half past five. Banner was snoring, and Morgan again tried to sleep but he couldn't. At five minutes to six, he got up and turned to wake the marshal. Banner was already sitting up.

"Evenin', Morgan." Banner stretched, stood up and pulled his arms back and forth to loosen up. "Touch o' roomatiz, I'd guess. This is the wrong job for an old man."

"Why don't you quit," Morgan asked.

"Not me! Jake Graybow quit. Next I heard, big New York newspaper payed his fare back east. Bill Cody put him in that Wild West show he does and Ned Bunline had him wrote up in ever' dime novel for the next three years."

"That so bad?"

"Found him broke an' drunk in some county home 'bout two years later. Sobered him up and he got hold of a gun and blew his brains out." Banner shook head back and forth. "No, sir, not me. When I go, I want it to be quick and clean." He pointed. "Right down there in the street, mebbe, or up in

Ouray. Wherever, whenever, I want to see it comin'
. . . not sneakin' up on me gradual."

Colorado Charlie Utter wasn't hard to find. He
had just sat down to a poker game when Banner
walked up. It was in one of the two big casinos at the
Hampton House, Silverton's biggest and best.

"Lo, Charlie."

"Well, I'll be damned . . . Ephram Banner. Hell, I
thought you was dead."

"Practical am, Charlie."

Charlie Utter was a stringbean of a man with a
beak nose and a deep scar that ran from just
beneath his right ear, along his lower jaw bone, and
ended beneath his chin. Charlie said it was a gift
from a Sioux warrior. When others told the story, it
was given to him by Crazy Horse. Charlie never
bothered to set the record straight either way.

Morgan noted Colorado Charlie's weapons. He
carried a Buntline special in a cut-out holster, waist
high. He also had a Colt Peacemaker tucked in his
waistband.

"Like to talk to you, Charlie, an' have you meet a
friend of mine. Son of a fella you knew once, you n'
Bill."

"Sure thing, Ephram. Lead the way."

The trio found a table in a semi-darkened corner
and Banner told Colorado Charlie what had
happened and why they were in Silverton. He ended
his story with a more formal introduction.

"Morgan here . . . Lee Morgan, well, he's the
offspring of Buckskin Frank Leslie."

"Hell fire!" Charlie smiled, broadly. "I knowed
your daddy real good. So did Bill. Tell you some-

thing, son . . . Frank Leslie was the coolest head I ever saw in a gunfight."

"That's a helluva statement," Morgan said, "considering who you rode with."

" 'Twas Bill Hickok what first said it. They throwed down on each other oncest. No shootin' o' course . . . but they throwed down."

"Who won?"

"Now that is a good one, son, a real good one. I was there an' I can't tell you." Morgan smiled. He was getting a history lesson about his father.

"Well, Charlie . . . you know who's here, you know why, and you know the reputations. It's not your fight, but Banner and I could use you."

"Charlie Utter don't work cheap, son . . . there's a price."

"Name it," Morgan said, surprised at the statement.

Colorado Charlie's face stretched into a big grin. "I git Charlie Hawks . . . jist me. Used muh name once up in Dakota territory. Got a bank loan from it. I had to pay it back. I owe him." Morgan laughed.

Charlie went back to his poker game. Banner told him he'd get word to him when the time came, and started back to the hotel with Morgan. As they were crossing the street, someone called Banner's name.

"Banner!" The marshal stopped, putting his hand up to stop Morgan from too hasty a move. The marshal turned, slowly. Morgan turned as well. "Got yourself a kid deppity now, have you?"

"Hello, Largo."

"You lookin' fer *me*?"

"Don't flatter yourself, Largo. My dodger on you says five hundred. You must have slipped a lot lately. Hell, Quint Yokley's worth twice that."

"You won't live to collect it, no matter what it is."

"Mebbe, mebbe not, Largo. But why don't we find out. Sunday mornin'?"

"What's the matter with right now?"

"I'm here with mister Morgan to bring in four men, not one."

"Morgan?"

"Lee Morgan, Largo. Pinkerton man."

Largo grinned. "*Pinkerton.*" He laughed. "Hell, Banner, I've put more Pinkerton men in a buryin' box than you could count. That all the help you got?"

"Show up Sunday, Largo, and find out."

"Show up where?"

"Empty lot next to the mercantile two blocks over. Seven o'clock."

"You know who else is in town?"

Morgan answered that one. "We know. And you tell Doc Henry if he tries runnin' out again, I'll come after him fast. Got nothing to hold me up this time."

"One more thing, Largo . . . just to keep it official. You and Quint Yokley, Charlie Hawks, and Doc Henry Jared are all under arrest. If you decide to change your mind about Sunday . . . I'm at the *Mother Lode* hotel." Marshal Banner turned and walked on. It took Morgan a moment to catch him.

"I admire your style, Banner," Morgan said, "but times have changed. If Doc Henry—or any of those men riding with him—get a chance at back shooting one of us before Sunday, they'll do it." Banner said nothing, but held the door open for Morgan. Finally, Morgan entered. Upstairs, he had more to say. "Don't ignore me, Banner."

"I wasn't ignoring you, Morgan. Just pondering what you said."

"Then you agree?"

"Not completely. Oh, times have changed but *men* haven't . . . least ways, men like these. Anyways, we'll do somethin' about it . . . tonight!"

"What?"

Banner smiled. "Now that's where you're showin' you're no lawman. We got a town here, Morgan, a whole town. They won't fight, but they like honor. Tonight, I'll show you what I mean."

Banner found Morgan in the saloon downstairs at just after eight o'clock. "Take your gun upstairs," Banner said, "and I'll meet you in the lobby."

"What?"

"Do it, Morgan. Trust me." Morgan looked down. Marshal Banner wasn't wearing a gun. A few minutes later, Morgan appeared in the lobby, still frowning at the latest request of the old lawman.

"Where we headed?" Morgan asked.

"The Hampton House. Friday night, my guess'd be that all four of 'em are there."

The main casino at the Hampton House was so crowded it was difficult to move through it. Morgan noted the smile on Banner's face. It grew even larger when he spotted the four men. He nudged Morgan and pointed.

"Let's walk on over."

"What about Charlie Utter?"

"We'll save him fer Sunday. Besides, I already got word to him where and when to meet us."

Morgan didn't like any of what was going on. He was beginning to question why he'd even agreed to it. He respected Banner, and he'd asked for the marshal's help. But this wasn't what he had in mind.

"Evenin', gents," Banner said, casually. Doc Henry spotted Morgan and leaped to his feet, his chair clattering across the floor behind him. "He's not wearin' a gun, Jared. Me neither." Suddenly the noise in the casino was gone. Morgan slowly looked around. Nearly everyone was looking at the group of men.

"What the fuck you want, marshal?"

"Got to thinkin' maybe Largo's memory wouldn't be so good anymore. Decided to deliver my own message."

"Sumbitch! We got your message."

"Well, just in case, Doc . . . I'll give it to you again. The four of you are under arrest. If you want to turn yourselves in, I'm at the Mother Lode hotel. If you don't, I'll see you Sunday mornin' at the lot beside the mercantile. If you try to ride out before that . . . I'll gun you down on sight."

Doc Henry's Colt was in his hand. He was pointing it at Marshal Banner's belly. A voice from out of the crowd got Doc's attention.

"We don't take kindly to shootin' unarmed men in Silverton."

Another voice. "And with the sheriff gone, be hard to control folks what got mad."

Banner smiled at Doc. "Use it, Jared . . . right now. In ten minutes you'll be hangin' from a rafter."

"You sumbitch!" Doc slowly holstered his gun.

"See you Sunday, Doc," Banner said.

Banner and Morgan moved to the bar. Morgan eyed the old lawman and half grinned. "That was about the slickest bunch of work I ever saw, marshal." Even as he spoke, Morgan could hear nearby men taking bets on the outcome of Sunday's showdown. "The only thing I would have done different was buy myself a little edge . . . just in case."

Banner smiled and pointed to the balcony. Morgan looked up and saw Charlie Utter with a shotgun. Charlie waved and walked away.

17

Saturday disappeared like a puff of smoke in a brisk wind. Morgan lay on his bed, wide awake. It was just after one thirty, Sunday morning. Marshal Ephram Banner was breathing the heavy breath of a deep sleep, but Morgan was worried. Not scared . . . worried. He'd come after Doc Henry Jared. No matter what Banner had accomplished, Morgan knew Doc Henry. If there was a way out, he'd find it.

Morgan jumped. The Colt flew into his hand in response to a light knock at the door. Marshal Banner was awake.

"I'd answer it, Morgan. Don't think those other fellas would bother with knockin'." Morgan walked over and opened the door.

"Don't be mad with me," Beth said. Morgan was, but it didn't last long. "I got off the stage an' telegraphed Creede. I waited for an answer. If Billy wasn't comin', I was gonna leave."

"He is coming?"

"I'm already here, Morgan." Billy stepped out of

the shadows in the hallway.

"Not for long," Morgan said. "When I first tried to contact you, things were different."

"Yeah," Billy said, "I guess they wuz." Morgan looked surprised at the firmness in Billy's tone. "Beth tol' me what she done with ya. She's her own woman, an' I'd rather it wuz you than some."

"There's more to it than that," Morgan said.

"Doc Henry an' three gunnies."

"Not gunnies, Billy, not these men. Charlie Bojack was a gunny. So was Cully and Hightower. These men are gun fighters. Professional shootists. That's how they live."

"Morgan," Billy said, stepping into the room. "I'm here. I won't be leavin' 'til they're dead or I am. You can keep me from comin' with you, but you can't keep me from bein' there. 'Less'n you plan to call me out right now."

"That what you plan on doin', Morgan?" Morgan turned. A quizzical expression crossed his face. The question came from Banner.

"No," Morgan said. "It isn't. And this isn't any of your business, marshal."

"I walk into a gunfight with a man, ever'thing he does is my business. You take the boy out now, you'll feel it in the morning. You run 'im off and he shows up, you'll feel it. Only place he *can* be is with us. You thought he was good enough before. What's changed?"

"Shit!" Morgan said. "A helluva lot of things have changed."

"Name just one that'll help keep us alive in the mornin', 'cept for this boy bein' here and offerin' his guns." Morgan felt his face getting warm. He was angry, mostly with himself. He knew better than to tie himself to somebody, anybody, before a fight. He turned and looked at Beth. She smiled.

"Billy could be laid out on slab board eight hours from now. Men here will be collecting money over his corpse."

"I know," she said, "but my momma always said Billy had to earn what he wanted. He wants to be with you in the mornin'. Hasn't he earned that Morgan? Hasn't he?"

Colorado Charlie Utter was just finishing a two inch thick cut of beef, four eggs, and coffee when Morgan walked into the dining room. He saw Charlie, shook his head in disbelief and then glanced at the clock. It was 6:20.

"Coffee, Morgan?"

"Yeah." Morgan took several sips of coffee, eyeing Charlie's shotgun. He thought it looked odd. "What make is your scatter-gun, Charlie?"

"My own, mostly. Fat part there, near the stock," he grinned, "holds an extra shell. Got a roll lever in it. Fire both barrels an' it rolls that third shell into the empty chamber. Left chamber if'n they're both empty."

"Ever used it?"

"Yeah . . . several times. Works right nice."

"Surprises a few people too, I'd guess." Charlie grinned and nodded.

"Maybe this mornin'."

"We've got a fourth, Charlie . . . kid named Billy Frye. Rode with Doc Henry for awhile. No more. He's good, real good."

"But not good enough, Morgan, is that it?"

"I don't think so."

"Run 'im next to me. I'll keep an eye on 'em fer ya. He sees you watchin' i'm, he's li'ble to git all choked up at the wrong time."

"Thanks, Charlie."

At 6:40, Marshal Ephram Banner and Billy Frye came down stairs. Banner gave a black boy named Zeb a dollar to run over to the site of the meeting and see if the gunmen were waiting. He returned after five minutes later and reported that all four of them were there.

"Let's go," Banner said. The four walked abreast, Charlie at one end with his scatter-gun and then Billy, Banner and Morgan. Silverton's streets were empty, vacant even of the usual drunken miners who never got back to their sleeping quarters. Faces could be seen peering from windows and hands pulled back window shades briefly, but no one wanted to run the risk of being on the streets and getting caught up in a running gunfight if anything went awry.

The foursome turned the corner and half way down the block Marshal Banner said, "They'll spread on us so I figger we'd be best to go man on man."

"Who's the best man there?" Billy asked. He seemed nervous, edgy. Banner knew the boy was scared.

"Be a toss up, Billy, 'tween Doc Henry an' Quint Yokley. I'll take Quint." Banner turned and looked at Morgan. "Doc?" Morgan nodded. "Then Charlie gets the scatter-gun an' you take Largo."

"Yessir," Billy said.

"I'd like to take at least one of 'em in. I won't ask

ya to shoot that way, but if one goes down an' can't do no more . . . try to leave 'im breathin'."

At the corner of 3rd Street, the four men stopped. Half a block east was the vacant lot. They could see Doc and the others lined up, waiting.

"Haven't known any of ya too long," Banner said, " 'cept Charlie. Wish I had."

"Let's plan to see to it you get to know us better," Morgan said. The wily old marshal smiled and nodded.

"Let's get it over with."

Silverton was no stranger to such confrontations. There had been many men who fought one another, sometimes with guns, sometimes with knives . . . even bare-handed. Most were obscure gamblers, gunnies, or just plain mean. There had also been a few big showdowns; the day Bill Hickok and Charlie Utter faced down the Butcher brothers was one of them. Another day, on a Sunday, Doc Holliday shot and killed a bounty hunter by the name of Joe Hedley. John Ringo visited Silverton and shot a young hot-head whose name was never known. But none of those measured up to what was about to happen. The only participant in this fray who had no reputation was Billy Frye. If he survived it, the mark it would place on him was one he would carry to his grave.

"I'm givin' you one final chance," Banner said. As he spoke, Colorado Charlie, Billy Frye, and Morgan moved away from him, eyeing the four men opposite them and positioning themselves accordingly.

"You'll git a trial by a jury of your peers an'

sentenced according to their findings. I'm here to arrest you, and the men with me are duly authorized deputies. If you resist arrest, we'll defend ourselves."

"Pretty speech, Banner," Largo said. "Now you'll have to back it up."

Quint Yokley didn't wait. He drew and fired as fast as any man present had ever seen. No one else moved except Marshal Ephram Banner. Morgan was near enough to hear the crack of bone as the bullet struck home. It came just after Banner had fired his own gun. Banner's face contorted with pain and then a ripple ran through his big-boned frame. His right leg wobbled and gave way and he dropped, landing on his right side. His gun flew from his hand. Quint Yokley had clearly beaten the old lawman, but he was more fast than accurate. Quint was already dead. Still falling, but already dead. The slug hit him in the forehead.

What happened immediately after that not even an eye-witness could have stated for sure, let alone a participant. One voice was heard, that of Doc Henry Jared. He spoke his favorite word.

"Sumbitch!" Doc drew amid the roar of a shotgun discharging. He levelled his weapon at Morgan's chest, allowing for Morgan's possible draw and crouch. Doc's shot went wild. Morgan's bullet just nicked the barrel of Doc's gun, not by design but by accident. The fluke saved both their lives. Morgan proved the fastest and escaped unscathed. Doc Henry's left side was bleeding, he had two broken ribs and he was out of the fight.

Colorado Charlie Utter cut loose, low, with both barrels of his scatter-gun. The shot struck Charlie

Hawks in both legs . . . about knee high. Colorado had fired the weapon with his right hand, from his hip. Simultaneously, he drew the Peacemaker from his waistband with his left hand.

Charlie Hawks was one of the best, and his speed was even greater than Utter's action with the shotgun. Colorado Charlie took a slug in the right shoulder. The Peacemaker's bullet shattered Hawks' right elbow as he was falling. He'd be walking on crutches for a long time, and he'd never fire a gun again with his right hand. Colorado Charlie stayed on his feet. He knew in an instant that he wouldn't be able to help Billy Frye.

But Billy didn't need help. Largo Johnson had Billy pretty well sized up. He toted two guns for show, but he was a right hander. Largo was not the fastest of the four . . . but he was clearly the most accurate. He aimed for Billy's right-hand holster, and he beat the kid by just a hair's breadth. The thing Largo didn't expect was that Billy used his left-hand draw. He'd been practicing harder on it to develop his accuracy. He killed Largo with a single shot, but went down from the spinning force of Largo's shot when it struck Billy's other gun.

Morgan kept his gun levelled at the spot where the four men had been. "Billy dead?" he asked Utter.

Charlie looked down. He saw movement. "You dead, boy?"

"Hardly," Billy said. He got to his feet. "Damn. He ruint muh rig."

Morgan could see Doc Henry trying to get up. He got to his knees and a violent cough wracked his body. He spit, cursed and his arms gave way. He was finished. Charlie Hawks was beginning to feel the pain. He was doubled into the fetal position and holding his knees with his good arm, howling at the top of his lungs.

Morgan holstered his gun and knelt next to Marshal Banner. "How bad?"

"Hip bone . . . whole damn thing's busted from the feel of it." Banner twisted his head, grimacing with each movement. He managed a twisted smile. "But I'll live, Morgan, I'll live."

"Quint Yokley didn't," Morgan said.

"That's how I played it."

A crowd had gathered. Even from the street, it was obvious who had come out on top. The town doctor pushed his way through the little knot of people. He was carrying his black bag and was followed closely by the town undertaker.

"Three for immediate doctoring," Morgan said. Colorado Charlie had already waved the doctor away. The bullet had gone clean through. "Marshal Banner first." The doctor nodded.

"Only two to be fit fer a box?"

"For now," Morgan said, "but there'll be a trial . . . and I'd guess a hangin'."

Wagons were brought up and the wounded and dead, save for Colorado Charlie, were carted off. He walked away with the crowd. Morgan and Billy Frye stood alone, only the breeze making any sound as it whistled through the boards of an old building.

Billy finally walked over to where Morgan was standing. He'd taken his rig off and it was looped over his shoulder. "Well, Mister Morgan, did I qualify?"

"You did, Billy." Morgan looked the kid square in

the eye. Billy hadn't seen that particular look on Morgan's face before. "Now you don't have to qualify anymore." Morgan pointed to Billy's rig and continued, "You got it off . . . leave it off."

Billy looked down and smiled a weak smile. "Ya know," he said, "I was kinda thinkin' that to muhself, Mister Morgan. Maybe 'bout takin' Beth and goin' home." He looked up. "Tryin' to figger a way to make a livin', but . . . but hangin' these up. This mornin' wasn't like I figgered it'd be. Muh feelin', I mean."

"It never is, Billy. You got a good idea there. Stick with it."

"An' you, Mister Morgan? What you gonna do?"

"Watch Doc Henry hang." Morgan paused in his answer. He looked north, smiled faintly, and then looked back at Billy. "Then mebbe I'll go home too. Back up Idaho way."

18

Charlie Hawks, still recuperating from Colorado Charlie's shotgun, was tried in *absentia* for a dozen or more crimes, none of them related to Doc Henry Jared. The evidence against him was overwhelming, but the jury showed some leniency when they learned that Charlie Hawks would never walk again.

He drew eight years, but the judge put him on probation. He ultimately turned to gambling, worked his way east and plied his trade on Mississippi river boats. Almost two years to the day after the shoot-out in Silverton, Charlie Hawks was shot dead. He was caught dealing from the bottom.

Doc Henry's trial was another matter entirely. It was moved from Silverton back to Creede on a change of venue. The whole town loved it. It was another boom, as good as any gold or silver strike ever found. Few incidents in Colorado's long and often inglorious history had drawn such attention or so much security. Creede even built a special cell to house him.

Colorado Charlie could really offer no direct

evidence against Doc. He left the judge with a deposition, and he left Colorado for his old stomping grounds in Deadwood, Dakota Territory. Morgan wondered if they'd ever meet again.

Morgan, Beth, and Billy returned to Creede even before Doc Henry was moved. Marshal Banner would be sufficiently recovered from his own wound to be there for the trial.

Morgan reined up in front of Molly's place, dismounted and just stood in the street. No one he'd talked to, not even Billy, had been able to supply any information about Molly's fate.

Morgan walked through the bat wing doors as he had done so many weeks before, expecting to have to check his guns. He saw a new man working security. The man walked over, smiled and said, "Welcome, Mister Morgan. Go on upstairs. I believe Miss O'Flynn is expecting you." Morgan smiled and went upstairs.

"Welcome back, Mahrgan." She walked to him, they hugged and she kissed him. "You know, I'd have been mighty angry with you if you'd gone an' got yourself killed."

"I wouldn't have been so happy about it myself," Morgan said. She poured them both a celebration drink and they sat down. "Trigg," Morgan said, softly . . . "I mean . . ."

"Sean? No, Mahrgan. He tried. God, he tried."

"He was a helluva man, Molly. I'm sorry."

"He wouldn't have had it any other way." Molly told him what had happened to her. When she finally regained consciousness, a cavalry patrol found her, wandering near the river.

"Emmy?" Molly shrugged.

"She was gone when I woke up. I didn't even think about her 'til later. The army said they never saw her. They made a thorough search too, for her and others. The valley, Doc's trail west . . . ever'where, Mahrgan. She just vanished. Maybe she was . . ."

"The Apaches?" Molly nodded. "Yeah, it's possible." Morgan stood up, kissed Molly again, softly. "I'll be around," he said, "if you need to talk."

Morgan walked to the army command post. There he learned that General Utley had succumbed to his wounds. Gangrene. Young Yates had over-stepped his authority and was back east facing a court martial. Morgan also learned about Senator Venable's role in the army's rescue efforts and the loss of both Pinkerton agents. Venable had returned to Denver, but planned to be in Creede for Doc Henry's trial.

The trial opened three months after the showdown in Silverton. Creede's hotels, boarding houses and saloons were packed full every day and night. Newspapers from as far east as Chicago were on hand to report the proceedings. Ned Buntline himself showed up.

Doc Henry wasn't present for the two opening days. They were devoted to recording the many depositions and opening statements. The defense attorney, who had been court-appointed, found himself the object of considerable scorn and more security than that surrounding Doc Henry himself.

Morgan was just entering the court house on the morning of the third day when he felt a hand tugging at his arm. He turned.

"Mister Morgan. I'm relieved to see you alive." It was Senator Venable. His face was thin and drawn, and dark patches were prevalent below his eyes.

"I'm sorry Senator. Emmy . . . I was told what happened."

"Some satisfaction will come from this trial, Morgan. I've never been a vengeful man . . . but," he sighed. "I want to watch this man fall through the trap door."

"He will, Senator."

"I'll have your money, Morgan, whatever you say . . . after the trial."

"We'll talk about it, Senator, when the time comes."

Morgan, Molly, Billy, and Marshal Banner sat together, just behind the table of the Mineral County Prosecuting Attorney. He was handling the courtroom work, but also present was a representative of the Colorado State Attorney General's office. There was a stir, then a murmuring, then some unruliness when finally Doc Henry Jared was led into the courtroom. He was bound in wrist and leg irons, and he looked thinner. But there was still the contempt, the look of a man certain he would once again escape death. There was no sign of the wound Morgan had inflicted.

The judge, Clayton Jonas Howell, was one of the most reputable of Colorado's Circuit. He was strict, stern of countenance, and would tolerate nothing less than absolute order in his court. He silenced the crowd with a stern warning and showed irritation at a last minute arrival. No one else paid any attention. Doc Henry started laughing at the judge's pleas. He too was reprimanded, and threatened with gagging. Sullen, he finally slumped into a chair.

Just before the noon recess, Judge Howell addressed himself to the defendant. "Get to your feet, Mister Jared, and come stand before the bench." Doc Henry was led from the table. He stood, looking up and grinning. "When we return from lunch, you will be taking the stand. I expect you do to so in proper dress and without shackles. Nonetheless, there will be deputies on either side of you. They have been ordered to shoot you should any trouble occur. Any man, yourself included, is entitled to a trial by jury and should be considered innocent until proven guilty. I hold to that concept with every fibre of my being." Now the judge leaned forward and pointed a finger in Doc's face. "If, however, there should be trouble out of you, or from someone outside this court, I will personally take it as a confession from you indicating your guilt and I will act accordingly. Is that clear, sir?"

"Clear enough, yer honor." The judge then banged the gavel and called for mid-day recess. He stood to leave the courtroom and everyone else stood as well. Doc Henry turned around and a voice broke the silence.

"I loved you. I hated the boredom of my life . . . and I *loved* you. I could have provided everything for us. You would never have had to rob again. But you . . . the women . . . your filthy debasement of my love . . . you bastard!" Heads had jerked to the center aisle. Deputies were frozen in their tracks at the sight of the gaunt, feminine figure in the man's clothing.

"Emmy," Senator Venable said to himself, "my

God!" He leaped up. "Emilia, no, for God's sake, no!"

Morgan leaped from his seat, the first person to move quickly, but even he was too late. Emmy Venable brought the pistol from beneath her vest, levelled it at Doc Henry, and began firing. One . . . two . . . three . . . four . . . Morgan dived toward her, but she leaped back.

"Sum . . . bi . . ." Two of the bullets struck Doc Henry Jared in the head. The fifth shot caught him in the chest and drove his body backwards into the judge's bench. It hung there a moment, his eyes wide open, his mouth still moving. Then it slid slowly down until he was in a sitting position. Another moment and the head dropped to the side. Doc Henry Jared was dead.

Emmy stepped back again, put the .45 to her temple and pulled the trigger. It had all happened in seconds. Women began to scream and several fainted. Senator Venable, pushing to reach his daughter, stiffened suddenly and grabbed at his chest. Morgan got to his feet and slipped out a side door to fetch the doctor.

Senator Venable survived his heart attack. He resigned his powerful post in Washington and lived out his years, quite a number of them, in the seclusion of his Denver mansion. Emmy Venable's funeral was one of the most attended in Denver's history.

Morgan was paid well for his role in ending Doc Henry Jared's reign of terror. In addition to the money from Venable, reward money poured in from a dozen sources. He gave much of it to Billy and

Beth Frye.

Marshal Ephram Banner returned to Ouray and continued as the chief territorial law officer with deputies carrying out the field work. The showdown in Silverton was Banner's last hurrah.

Even as Creede was returning to some measure of normality, word came about the fate of the renegade Naschitti. He had, once more, outwitted his army pursuers and fled to Mexico. A few months later, however, he and his small band were trapped by Federales and fought to the death.

By the time most of the complexities of Doc Henry's death had been settled, winter snows were falling daily on Creede. Morgan decided to stay the winter. He knew he wouldn't be lacking for warmth and comfort . . . Irish style.

Spring came all too soon. On the night before Morgan was to pull out, he had a late-night visitor. It was Molly's going-away gift to him . . . and he was certain it would do him for quite awhile. The next day, Morgan readied his gear and the roan and then rode back to Molly's. She came out to meet him.

"I won't be askin' you to write ta me. I did that before." She smiled, stood up on her tip toes and kissed him. "Will you ever come back, Morgan?"

"I'll come back Molly . . . someday." He mounted, smiled at her blown kiss, flicked the brim of his hat, and rode out. He headed north, up over Spring Creek Pass and on to Slumgullion pass. Many times he looked down from the high country and thought back about what had happened.

He spent a day in Lake City, a way station for the Gunnison-Creede stage line. There, he heard the story of an old mountain man caught last winter in the high country and found frozen to death. He rode out to the little burying plot. There were only seven head boards. The most recent simply read,

STONER

Just north of Lake City station, Morgan found an overhang. He walked out on the giant boulder and looked over the vast expanse of the Uncompahgre. It was beautiful, but it stirred something deep in his soul.

"Home," he said to himself. "Home to Idaho and the Spade Bit . . . just maybe." He'd often thought of it and wondered what his father would have said about Morgan's sale of it. Particularly after he lost the money from it in a crooked lumber deal.

There were no more Wanted posters on Lee Morgan. Venable had been as good as his word. And the Senator had said that if Morgan ever needed help, all he had to do was ask for it. If the new owners wanted to sell . . . if they would. A new life . . . a life with no guns. Just maybe. "Home," he said again.

Morgan got up, mounted the big roan gelding, and said his last goodbye to Winchester Valley.